The Den of
Forever Frost

BEARS OF THE ICE

The Den of Forever Frost

Book 2

KATHRYN LASKY

SCHOLASTIC INC.

It was a bright cold day in April, and the clocks were striking thirteen.

— George Orwell, *1984*

NORTHERN KINGDOMS

Hrath gar Mountains

Glauxian
Brothers Retreat

Lagoon
of Moss

Hrath gar Glacier

Pirates'
Lair

Bay of H

Stormfast
Island

Skunk Bear's
Cave

Grundensphyrr Firth

Bay of
Fangs

Encounter with
Rebel Bears

Everwinter Sea

Elsemere
Island

Ice Dagger

Dark Flow
Island

To the Southern Kingdoms

Sea of
Nunquivik

Narwhale
Rescue
✕

N'yrthghar Straits

h

Everwinter Sea

4.

3.

Stormfast
Island

2.

1.

1. Ice Crevasse Entrance
2. Pleek's Plonk exit crevasse
3. Uthermere Firth
4. Rumored location of the Den
   of Forever Frost

Prologue

"The red comet burns . . . ," Svenna heard the Mystress of the Chimes whisper. The bears had gathered on the parapets and balconies beneath the clock face and were looking up at the sky. Hurtling through the bitter cold night, the comet's red light bled across the Ice Cap of the Ublunkyn, staining the white pelts of the bears.

"And now the chaos begins," the Mystress of the Chimes muttered.

Svenna was surprised that the Mystress of the Chimes, one of the highest-ranking Timekeepers, would even whisper such dangerous words. She rarely disclosed her thoughts. She was a riddle, this fantastically beautiful she-bear Galilya, Mystress of the Chimes. Her elegant head was tipped back as she looked at the stars bathed in the red afterglow of the comet. Her fur, the whitest that Svenna had ever seen, was tinged pink. There was something unearthly about her eerie beauty. She was also deceptive and treacherous, as Svenna had discovered since serving in her den.

"Chaos? How so, Mystress?" Svenna asked cautiously.

Galilya regarded her sharply, as if it was Svenna's fault that she had ears and had overheard her.

"How so? Superstition, my dear! And sorcery!" She gave a strange chuckle that was more like a bark than a bear chuff. "Superstition embraced by sorcery, a dangerous union."

The words sent a chill through Svenna. The word *sorcery* sounded unnatural to Svenna, unbearlike. But the Ice Cap was an unnatural place. Bears did not behave like bears here.

Then the air was shattered with a terrible screeching. An immense shape plummeted down from the highest parapet toward the ice ramparts. Shrieks of horror erupted from every bear watching — except the Mystress of the Chimes.

"What . . . what is that?" Svenna asked.

"Was," the Mystress said calmly. "That *was* our Chronos."

"The Chronos? Ivor Ahknah?" Svenna was aghast. Her ears flattened against her head and she felt her guard hairs stiffen. The Chronos was the second-highest officer of the Timekeepers, just under the Grand Patek. Together they oversaw the sacred duties that kept the Ice Clock ticking flawlessly. They believed that by worshipping the clock, it would prevent the next Great Melting. Although Svenna knew this was nonsense, she'd learned the hard way what happened to bears who questioned the power of the clock.

"Yes, Ivor Ahknah."

"But he has been here forever." He had been revered by the Timekeepers. Why this violent end?

"Sometimes forever is too long." The Mystress sighed. "And what a mess to clean up." Turning crisply, the elegant bear walked into the darkness of an ice tunnel.

A hush had fallen over the Ice Clock. Then the voice of the Grand Patek rang out through the ice horn echoers.

"The great Chronos Ivor Ahknah is dead, as foretold by the arrival of the red comet, as written in *The Auspices of Celestial Events*. Long live the new Chronos, Torsenvryk Torsen."

This is a cursed place, Svenna thought. But she'd do what it took to survive.

Of all the kingdoms in all the world, from the Nunquivik to the Northern Kingdoms of Ga'Hoole, from Ga'Hoole to the place of the wolves in the Beyond, there was no bear more determined than Svenna. She'd do whatever necessary. She would kill. She would destroy the clock. She would give up her life if she had to, as long as she could die knowing that her cubs were safe.

CHAPTER 1

A World Unhinged

As the red comet soared through the darkness, turning the moon and the stars crimson, three young bears swam through the ice floes of the N'yrthghar Straits — Stellan and his sister, Jytte, and their friend Third. It was almost the time of the Dying Ice Moons, and these straits that connected the sea of Nunquivik with the Everwinter Sea of the Northern Kingdoms were filled with fragments of bobbing ice. As the cubs plied their way through the maze of broken bergs that stirred slowly in the currents, their thoughts converged on one thing: their quest, a desperate mission to save both Stellan and Jytte's mother and the threatened world of the bears.

Svenna had been captured by power-hungry bears called Timekeepers, who worshipped the Ice Clock and were trying to take over the bear kingdoms. Their brutal methods included seizing cubs, who were then sacrificed to the clock. The only reason Stellan and Jytte hadn't met this grisly fate was because Svenna had offered herself in their place. When they'd first learned this, Stellan and Jytte had been frantic to launch a rescue mission. But their beloved teacher, Skagen, had explained, "You can't free her until you free your own kind." By *own kind*, Skagen meant the honorable bears whose lives were threatened by these tyrants of the Ice Clock.

The only way to rescue Svenna was to break the clock and destroy the power of the Grand Patek, the ruler of the Ice Cap. To do that, they had to find their father, Svern — a famous rebel who'd long fought against the Timekeepers. But he had been missing for years. It was rumored that he had gone back to the Northern Kingdoms and possibly the legendary Den of Forever Frost.

"We're getting so close to our father. I can feel it!" Jytte said, her voice brimming with excitement.

It always disturbed Stellan slightly when his sister spoke this way. He knew she was eager to find the father they had never met, but their mission had become about so much more. "It's not just about finding Da. We have to convince him to help us break the clock, and then we actually have to *do* it." His voice sounded brittle to his own ears. But he was frightened. Behind the brittleness was a sob waiting to break like a cresting wave.

Jytte splashed the water with her paw. "Are you accusing me of not taking this seriously? You're not the only one who cares about our mission, Stellan."

"But *you* only seem to care about finding *Da*. This is so much bigger than that."

Third looked from Jytte to Stellan. The smallest of the three cubs often served as the peacemaker between the sister and brother. When Svenna had been taken by Roguer bears, her cubs were left with Third's mother, Taaka, as cruel a she-bear as ever walked the frozen lands. Stellan and Jytte had escaped, and finally Third, the runt of Taaka's litter, fled too.

"You're both right," Third said gently. "It's hard to separate Svern from this mission. But regardless of whether we find him, we have to remain focused on breaking the clock."

"He's near the Den of Forever Frost. He must be!" Jytte said hotly. She was convinced they'd find her father and refused to think otherwise. "Skagen said so."

"Skagen said he was most likely there, Jytte. Most likely." Stellan spoke in a soothing voice. He had to be patient with his impetuous sister, whose passion could be overwhelming.

"We're getting closer." She stopped swimming and tipped her head toward the sky. "Remember, Skagen said that these straits turned south and west and led into the firths — the firths where our mum and da came from. He showed us that on the maps."

The other two cubs paused to look up at the stars sparkling through the skin of the cloudless night.

"We're just south and west of the Svree star," Stellan said, lifting a paw toward one of the two stars that pointed north to the Nevermoves star. "Our guide star. The one Mum . . ." His voice dwindled as he recalled those nights before their mother had been taken. She'd begun to teach them about the stars and how one could use them to navigate through a territory unknown, a world they had never seen.

"They'll start to fade soon. Dawn will be coming. And our guide star will disappear," Third said.

"I'll race you to the dawn," Jytte yipped. She was always ready for a race.

"Ha!" Stellan said. "Then you'd be going backward. The dawn will be breaking behind us in the east. We're going west."

"Oh, Stellan. Don't be so . . . so . . . exact. I mean I'll race you until the light comes. Comes and eats the night." She tore off and began pulling her forearms through the water. A wake curled evenly off her rear paws.

Stellan had always envied his sister for her power in the water. Her rear paws were just right for boosting her speed, whereas one of his had a slight turn that made paddling difficult. The water curled off in a lopsided way.

Jytte swung her head around and looked at him with a slightly anxious expression. Anxious or sad? A dimness had veiled her eyes, as if she was recalling some sorrow or loss. Was she perhaps thinking of Skagen? Stellan wondered. His sister's moods could change so quickly. Although Skagen was a snow leopard, he had taught them nearly as much as their mother had. The beautiful creature had shown them how to read ancient maps, instructed them about timepieces, and told them about the Ice Clock where the Tick Tocks were sacrificed. "Remember, cubs," he had once said. "A clock is only a tool, invented by the Others — it is not a god to be worshipped."

"Are you all right, Jytte?" Stellan asked.

"I'm fine," she said in a cheerful voice that didn't quite match the wistful look in her eyes. If she had felt grief for Skagen, she would never betray it.

Racing ahead, Jytte glanced up at that pointer star Svree. Just to swim under its light now reflected on the glassy dark water excited her.

Svree had been the chieftain of the first Bear Council in the Den of Forever Frost, and the cubs' very own ancestor. Their mum had often referred to that period as the "time of the way of Svree" — an age of old traditions, and most important, the old stories and legends of the clan bears. That was what Jytte was racing toward — not a dawn but a time before time in a dawn they had only heard about. That time of Svree that was linked in all bears' minds to the noble bears of the Ice Star Chamber who gathered in the very depths of the Den of Forever Frost.

"Come on, Stellan!" Third shouted. "Remember Marven!"

Yes, Marven! Stellan thought gleefully as he swam past Jytte. Svree was not their only illustrious ancestor. There was also Marven, a hero from the time of the Great Melting, when most of the bear lands were awash with sea monsters. Marven, a renowned swimmer, had vanquished many of the savage dragon walruses who cut bloody swaths through the rising waters, killing thousands of bears.

"You beat me!" Jytte called ahead, breathing heavily. "Don't you ever complain to me again about how you can't keep your hind paws flat for ruddering." But Jytte laughed as she swam up to her twin brother and tugged playfully on his ear. "Wanna water wrestle?"

"No time for wrestling," Stellan said, pulling away. "Come on, Jytte, we have a mission. I think we're about to enter the firths where our mum and da came from. According to Skagen's maps, they lead to the Den of Forever Frost."

A loud crack suddenly split the air, and the cubs swiveled to look behind them. A huge iceberg had cleaved in half. It was close enough that they felt the disturbance in the water.

"Just another berg cubbing," Stellan said as he watched the two chunks of ice bobbling about in the dark water of the straits. The split was almost perfect, which made the two parts appear like the ice wings of some gigantic mythical bird.

"This passage is getting narrower and narrower. Soon even I won't fit." Third forced a chuckle, but Stellan was alert to the anxiety in his voice. This would not be a good place to be trapped. It didn't take much effort to imagine a vicious toothwalker, a descendant of the dragon walruses, swimming toward them.

"Now what do they call this sort of channel in Krakish?" Again, Third tried to sound cheerful and curious.

"A *byssenskitch*," Stellan said.

"Byssenskitch," Third repeated thoughtfully. He'd always felt that Stellan and Jytte were lucky to have a mother like Svenna who knew the language of their ancestors. His own mother, Taaka, had also come from the Northern Kingdoms, but she apparently had forgotten Krakish and only spoke Nunqui to him and his two siblings. However, there was more to fault about

Taaka than her language. She was foul tempered and the most unmotherly creature who ever lived.

The byssenskitch had narrowed enough to prohibit them from swimming side by side. Jytte took the lead, with Third behind her and Stellan behind Third.

The passage was studded with fractured sea ice threaded with the bluest water the cubs had ever seen. The pieces bobbled gently as the currents stirred beneath them. It was sometimes possible to climb out onto a large chunk and hop from one floating fragment to another.

"Ice hopping! I love it!" Third cried out. As the smallest cub, he was the most capable of landing on very small fragments, balancing for a split second, then skipping off to the next. They all paused for a moment and sat on individual fragments and looked about at this new landscape, this new country where Stellan and Jytte's parents had been born and raised.

One of Jytte's favorite things to do was imagine stories about her father. Svern must have been an incredibly brave bear to lead a rebellion to break the clock, even if he hadn't succeeded. Had he fought paw to paw with the horrific Roguer bears whose faces were crisscrossed with battle scars?

Jytte was not alone in imagining Svern. Stellan's mind also stirred with dreamlike images of this nearly mythic father they had only heard about. Skagen had told them of Svern's special talent. "He was a Yinqui, young'uns."

"A Yinqui?" Stellan had asked. "What's that?" This odd word only deepened the mystery surrounding their father. Was a

Yinqui a good thing or a bad thing? Could they ever hope to know their father as they had their mum?

"An ice listener. It's a strange talent. He could listen through ice. In short, spy on the Timekeepers at the clock." In his mind, Stellan pictured a bear with very large ears, one pressed to a slab of ice, his eyes keen and sparkling as he picked up enemy chatter.

The passage had widened a bit, and the fragments of pack ice had diminished and cleared the watery path. The three cubs looked about in wonder as they swam. This land was much different from where they had come. They could see now that it was mountainous country with tall, jagged peaks scraping the sky. The flanks of these mountains pitched steeply down to the sea.

Third began to observe the animal life that skittered across the ice near the edge of the straits. A small troop of lemmings ambled over a shrinking patch of snow. He noticed that the blinding-white pelt of a fox had begun to turn darker in anticipation of the coming snowless days. Flying above, the tiny birds known as blue widgies had started to lose their winter plumage and were now sprouting brownish feathers for spring.

"It's different here," Third said, relishing the unfamiliar, for it confirmed that he was entering a world far from that of his savage mother, Taaka. Third was still plagued by his dreams of her, and the farther he could get, the safer he would feel. For Stellan and Jytte, this was a journey toward something dear to them — their father — but for Third, it was a journey away from something he had loathed — his mother.

"Even the clouds are strange," Jytte said. "Look, they're turning purple. Have you ever seen a purple cloud?"

"No," Third replied, his voice suddenly taut.

Stellan looked up. He didn't like Third's tone, nor did he like the color of those early morning clouds. The wind abruptly switched direction, and then he felt a slight pull on his port hind paw. Was this one of the mysterious currents he had heard about from Skagen? The lemmings were beginning to race wildly toward a precipice of ice. A fox suddenly stopped, seemingly frozen to the ground, and the blue widgies were pitching randomly in the sky, tossed by supercharged gusts of wind.

"Look at that!" Jytte shouted as she pointed. The sky that had been a misty blue, tinged with the purple of the gathering clouds, was starting to fracture. Spikes of lightning split the blue, sparks danced off peaks, and a juddering wind rattled the ice-sheathed flanks of the mountains. The mountain themselves seemed to quake as flashes of lightning streaked through the sky. A torrent of water cleaved one mountain, and a river that seconds before had been invisible raced toward them, sweeping the cubs to the sea.

In a single moment, the world became unhinged. Jytte felt the water's power surging around her, through her, beneath her. *I am being devoured!* The force of the river sucked the cubs under. Stellan saw Third thrashing in the water and grabbed the smaller cub with his mouth. As he struggled to fight the current, he searched desperately for Jytte but couldn't see her.

Stellan's lungs began to burn, but he couldn't open his mouth to breathe without losing his hold on Third.

After all they had been through, how could it end this way? Where was Jytte? He had to breathe. He felt as if his lungs would burst. And yet he could not swim up to the surface. There was no surface. He was being dragged down, down, down to the very bottom of this suffocating darkness. There was something pressing on his back. A weight of some sort. But, dizzy and exhausted, he felt himself losing his grip on Third. He didn't want to, but he had no choice. Everything was a confusing swirl of pain and shadow. Just as Third began to drift away, Stellan felt a peculiar surge of energy swelling beneath him. He began to soar toward the surface, soar like a bird in the sky, except he had no wings. He was being propelled by a power many times stronger than him, stronger than any bear on earth.

The darkness of the water faded, suffused by a fragile blue light. He broke through the surface with a gasp, and a moment later found himself awash on a shelf of ice of a jagged steep shore. Stellan wrenched his head to the side to see two sodden lumps lying nearby — breathing! Jytte and Third. It seemed miraculous. It *was* miraculous! All together and alive!

Third had flopped near Stellan's feet, his small chest rising up and down rhythmically. Jytte was next to Third, her eyes just opening. She coughed a bit, as if trying to get out a word or two. Then tried again.

"Stellan." She gasped as she saw a small stain of blood on his fur. "Your back! I clawed the fur right off your back. You're bleeding. Not much, though." *So that was the weight he had felt on his back*, thought Stellan — his sister. "Does it hurt?"

"No, no, not at all." He let his eyes feast on the sight of his sister, alive and well. Third was now conscious, and beginning to sit up on his haunches as he rubbed his eyes. They all looked at one another in wonder. Jytte was patting herself as if to make sure she had not lost any limbs.

"You saved us, Stellan," Third said, his voice ragged.

"No, not me. It was something else," Stellan said, still slightly dazed.

"What do you mean?" Third asked.

"I was just about to let go of you, Third. I had you in my mouth, but I couldn't breathe and then some . . . some . . . I don't know how to explain it — some force, a mysterious force — a current, maybe . . ." He looked at the river, the new river that flowed into the sea. The byssenskitch that they had been swimming through was no longer. It seemed as if the land had been rearranged completely.

"How will we ever find our way?" Jytte asked, seized with a sudden and new panic. "How will we ever find Da?"

"Don't worry, Jytte," Stellan said, trying to muffle the quake in his voice as he looked around with dismay. All the plans they'd laid with Skagen had suddenly become worthless.

"Don't worry!" Her words came out like a high-pitched squeak. "The world has played a dirty trick on us. How will we ever find the Den of Forever Frost?" She looked about. It was as if this unknown force had deliberately scrambled the geography. "Everything has changed from the maps," Jytte fumed.

Third looked at Stellan. "Let me climb onto your shoulders, Stellan. I'll be able to see better." Stellan crouched down and Third scrambled up.

"Now stand up as tall as you can," Stellan said.

"See anything?" Jytte asked anxiously.

Third didn't respond for several seconds. "This river ends in a sea that I think might be the Everwinter Sea but . . ."

"But what?" Stellan asked. If they didn't spot something they recognized, they'd never find the Den of Forever Frost.

"I see something else." Third squinted as he stared ahead at the now-unfamiliar landscape. New channels and paths had opened up between the fractured ice, revealing sharp objects piercing the surface. "That's strange," Third murmured.

"What?" Stellan asked, more urgently this time.

"I can see something long and sharp, but they aren't tusks of toothwalkers."

"I hope not!" Jytte exclaimed. Stellan felt a twinge in his haunch. He had been stabbed by the tusk of a toothwalker in a skirmish over a beluga whale.

"They're thinner, sharper than a toothwalker tusk."

"Well, what is it? What are you looking at?" Stellan asked, the ache in his haunch now throbbing.

"I'm not sure," Third replied, staring at the open water. By this time the surface of the water bristled with white ivory needles. A flock of small birds swooped down, then darted straight up again, as if suddenly aware of how close they had come to being impaled. The herd of needles began to move closer toward the ice shelf on which the cubs were perched. A peculiar clicking noise stippled the air. The sound was oddly familiar to Stellan and he instantly relaxed. *This* was the peculiar force that had propelled him to the surface.

"They're whales," Stellan whispered. "These are the creatures who saved us."

The whales swam toward the cubs, dipping in and out of the water. The ivory needles — their tusks — were gleaming and tapered. As the whales came closer, the cubs could see that the needles were spiraled. The creatures waved them about slowly in the soft light. It was a mesmerizing spectacle. And then the whales began to blow sprays of water that spangled the air. Stellan whispered, "Nar . . . they are Nar. They saved us."

"They were the mysterious force?" Third asked.

"Yes. They picked you up when I ran out of breath and thought I had dropped you at the very bottom of the sea."

"Yes!" Jytte exclaimed. "Mum told us that the word 'nar' in old Krakish meant noble. These are noble whales. Narwhals."

At that moment, one of the magnificent silvery-skinned creatures broke through the water and tapped the edge of the ice shelf with its spiraled tusk.

And that was all. The creature turned and swam off like a water-borne comet in a liquid night. The three cubs were silent for several moments as a calm stole over them. Stellan turned to Jytte. He put a paw on her shoulder. "We'll find the Den of Forever Frost, Jytte. We'll find our da. I just know it."

CHAPTER 2

A Warning Wrapped in a Riddle

Stellan slipped off the ice shelf and into the water. Jytte and Third followed. The Everwinter Sea bobbled with floes of ice torn loose from the flanks of the mountains during the strange storm, but there was no sign of the narwhals. Indeed, the only sounds they heard were the cracks and creaks of winter ice splintering, as spring had definitely arrived and summer would soon follow.

"I say there!" a small voice cried out as the cubs swam along the edge of one floe. Jytte's ears twitched. Was it actually a voice or just little squeaks of the ice? Ice could squeak a bit when it was about to splinter.

"Who says there?" Jytte asked.

"Me." The voice was creaky and brittle, and seemed to come directly from the ice itself. *Talking ice? Ridiculous!* Jytte told herself.

Third too had heard the voice and sensed that there might be a creature, a very tiny one, talking in its sleep as it wandered through a disturbing dream. The idea sent chills through Third, for he himself had wandered far in his dreams — not simply his dreams but others' dreams as well. He was what some called a dreamwalker, more commonly thought of as having second sight.

"Breathe on me," the voice whispered.

"What?" Jytte stopped swimming and began treading water. She scanned the edge of the floe, looking for the source of that creaky voice.

"Here, over here. No . . . more . . . talk . . . my head might break . . . off . . . just breathe on me."

I am breathing, Jytte thought as her eyes scanned the icy embankment. Then she noticed a little greenish head with bulging eyes encrusted in ice crystals peering out at her.

"Impossible" Jytte gasped as one of the figure's eyes began to blink.

"Oh, there is nothing, absolutely *nothing*, like the draft of a two-consonant blend! They just melt me," the creature said passionately.

"What are you talking about?" Jytte watched as the strange animal began to emerge from its frosty armor. It was not even half the size of her paw and was an odd greenish color.

"Had you exclaimed with a diphthong, for example blurted out 'oi!' Or 'ouch,' or 'ooh' . . . it wouldn't have worked. I wouldn't have melted. But you said 'impossible,' thank goodness."

"What's a diphthong?" Jytte asked.

"Who are you talking to?" Third asked. He and Stellan had just swum up and begun treading water.

Jytte turned to them. "I'm actually not sure."

"*Lithobates sylvaticus,*" said the creature.

"What?" Stellan exclaimed, confused by both the string of sounds and the small, strange creature who'd produced it.

"Ah, that did it, good fellow! That last blast from your powerful lungs freed me." Indeed, the small animal's sheath of ice was melting quickly from the warm exhalation of Stellan. It now hopped down the embankment ledge closer to the water.

"I am, as I just said, *Lithobates sylvaticus.* That is my species name. It means wood frog. But you may simply call me Sylvia."

"Wood frog or word frog?" Jytte asked, her mind swirling with new words.

"Oh, a little of both, but let's not get too technical. Anyway, I sensed you coming. I needed you early."

"You needed *us*? What for?" Third asked.

"I needed you before true summer. I am, in one sense, a frog for all seasons. But it is not yet true summer. In fact, it's a false spring. Had I tried to break out of my ice coffin, I would have most likely broken off a limb. Or in this case, my head."

"Your coffin?" Jytte asked. She wasn't sure she liked the sound of that word. "What is that?"

"My death box, my casket, my sarcophagus . . . or as we creatures who are suspended in deep hibernation call it, my *hibernaclum*, an ice tomb." Now Jytte was certain she didn't like that word.

"These are words we've never heard," Third said.

"They are death words," the frog replied calmly.

"But you are alive," Third pressed as Stellan and Jytte looked on in wonder.

"But once I was dead."

"Dead *once*?" Jytte blinked. "I thought one could only die one time. Once and for all."

"You speak in riddles," Stellan said. He tried in vain to grasp what this creature was — dead? Alive? In between? No, that was simply impossible.

"Indeed, I do speak in riddles. You see, my kind dies every winter. We freeze. Our blood does not stir. Our eyeballs are skimmed with ice and our hearts stop."

Jytte eyes grew huge with amazement. "You mean really and truly stop?"

"Absolutely. The last beat was on the fourth night of the Moon of the Just Ice. And here it will be in at least two moons, the Moon of the First Hatch."

"These are moons we've never heard of," Third said, frowning with confusion. In the land the cubs had left, the moons were named after the prey they hunted — the seal moons, the halibut moons.

"Of course you haven't. You're not a frog."

"And then you die after the Just Ice moon," Third said. He could not help but wonder what it felt like to be dead, then awaken. Or was it awakening and not being born for a second time? Did such a creature have to learn everything all over again? How to walk — no, not walk — swim again, hop, whatever they did.

"And then I die." Sylvia nodded her head, or as much as a neckless creature could nod its head.

"But now you're alive. Again," Third said. "It's the again part that confuses us."

"If I had I tried to break out of the ice too early, I might have broken off a limb, and then I would have been good as dead. Dead forever."

"Why would you ever break out before it was time?" Third asked.

"A compulsion, a pressure, an urge, an impulse . . . That is why I asked you to breathe on me, exhale a vigorous windy draft. A good robust 'wh' produces a great gust. Your warm breath has freed me."

"To do what?" Stellan asked.

"I already told you I am a riddle, a life wrapped in death, death wrapped in ice. My blood does not flow, my heart never beats, and yet dreams stir within me. Dreams unfinished, dreams barely started. They would be as shattered as my body and would go a-splinter. That is what our kind calls it when we defy the ice rules and break from our ice caskets. We often splinter." Suddenly a big tear began to roll from the little creature's bulging eyes.

"You're crying!" Third gasped in alarm. "Oh, frog, why are you crying?"

"I had a dream of my mate. I fear . . . I fear . . . he might have gone a-splinter."

"And if your mate has broken out early, what will happen?" Jytte asked. "Will you find him?"

Sylvia sighed deeply. "Parts, only parts. A leg here, another there . . ."

"Can he be mended?" Jytte asked.

"Possibly, if it's not too late. That's why I must go now. No more time for talk. Sorry. But thank you . . . thank you from the bottom of my newly beating heart."

And with that, Sylvia, freshly thawed from her ice tomb, sprang off into the clear blue air. "Farewell!" she cried as she flew over their heads, as graceful as a wingless bird.

"A riddle indeed!" Third murmured.

CHAPTER 3

Rumors of Svern

Jytte set her eyes on a horizon that was now jumbled with chunks of ice and a jigsaw-fractured frozen sea. "I wished we'd thought to ask Sylvia where we are," she said with a sigh. "Or at least asked her how to find the Den of Forever Frost."

"But would a frog know about that?" Third asked. "The Den of Forever Frost is a bear place."

"I think," Stellan began slowly, "I think we need to remember what those maps we studied with Skagen looked like."

Jytte scowled. "The maps would be useless even if we did have them. Nothing looks the same."

"But the stars are the same," Third said. "They can guide us to the Den of Forever Frost."

Jytte looked over her shoulder as they swam. "But it's midday. Do we have to wait for the stars to return?"

"Of course not! There *are* stars!" Stellan boomed. His voice was filled with new energy.

"Where?" Jytte challenged.

"The sun. The sun is a star. We know that. Mum told us so. The sun is the only one that shines during the day. And we know that the sun rises in the east and sets in the west. And we know that the Den of Forever Frost is southwest of the straits we swam through."

"But how far west? We might miss it if we just keep going west." The despair in Jytte's voice was clear.

"The coastline might have changed, but there are islands with roots to the very bottom of this sea. Do you remember Skagen showing us Stormfast Island on his map? He said it was called Stormfast because it holds fast to the seafloor through storms. If we pass that island, we'll know we have gone too far," Stellan said confidently. "So we have the sun. We have the island, and when night falls, we'll have the stars."

Jytte nodded ever so slightly. Her brother was right. Not all of the time. But some of the time. And in the end, didn't they both want the same thing? To find their father, stop the clock, and rescue Mum. But as Jytte scanned the coastline that resembled nothing they'd seen on Skagen's maps, none of that seemed possible.

"This has all the markings of a firth," Third said. "Remember Skagen told us that a firth is a channel of water that connects a bay with a smaller body of water like a pond or a lake. The currents are generally slow-moving, causing firths to freeze earlier. And do you feel how the current here has slowed?" The cubs stopped swimming and began treading water lightly. "Do you?" Third asked. The cubs had tipped back their heads as they suspended themselves in the water and concentrated.

"And that up there!" exclaimed Jytte. "Has all the markings of a spotted owl." A bird had silently emerged from a low cloudbank. One of Jytte's favorite lessons from Skagen had been learning how to identify various kinds of owls. Some were spotted. Some were barred. Some had tufts on their heads called horns. Some were big like the great grays, and some, the elf and the pygmy owls, were very tiny.

But what really fascinated Jytte was the silence of owls' flight and the speed with which they killed. Skagen had told them that from the clouds, an owl could hear the heartbeat of a mouse beneath the snow. Owls seemed as different from bears as any earthbound creature could be. Jytte felt that if, after she died, she could be born one more time, have just one more life, she would choose to be an owl.

High above, a spotted owl named Cleve soared on a billowing draft of air. Tipping his wings to port, he began to carve a slow turn. Fragments of the bears' conversation drifted up to him. He angled his head ever so slightly, first this way, then that. His unevenly placed ear slits began to home in on the talk. Sound traveled well in this dry air, and his slightly concave facial disc scooped their words from the breeze.

"Must be that way . . . ," one cub said, pointing toward the Bay of Fangs.

"It's a firth," said the other.

"But which one? The right one?"

Right one, thought Cleve. *What are they looking for?* They weren't hurt, that was all he knew. And that was good. So many of the cubs coming down from the Nunquivik had been terribly wounded. Glaux knew what they did to them up there. And these weren't bear rebels. Too young.

He had to get back. He was late from this surveillance flight and due to report in the parliament at the Great Tree.

He soared straight up and dissolved into the thick cloudbank directly overhead. The last words he picked up were "looks like a firth to me." It was the voice of a young female. "Firths can be connected to the Den of Forever Frost."

"But only one," said another voice, that of a male. "Only one is connected to the Den of Forever Frost, Jytte."

Now, whyever, thought Cleve, *would they want to know about that place? Ancient history!*

Jytte tipped her head back farther as she tracked the owl's flight until it vanished into a cloud. "He's gone," she whispered. There was a mournful tinge to her voice.

"It's as if the clouds swallowed the owl," Stellan replied as the cubs climbed out of the water, onto the ice.

"I wanted to watch it longer. Did you see how it moved its wings?" Jytte stood up and spread out her front legs and tipped them this way and the other. "I wonder what it's like to have feathers instead of fur?" she mused.

"Hey!" Third said abruptly. "Look what's coming our way."

"Oh no!" Stellan felt a chill run through him as the shapes of four bears appeared in the distance. "Roguers?"

"I don't think so," Third said, sounding more curious than frightened.

As the bears came into focus, Stellan began to tremble. "But I see blood on . . . on . . ." The Roguer bears often emblazoned their chests with the blood of their prey. Proudly they would stride about with it as a wanton display of their power.

"On his shoulder. Not across his chest," Jytte replied. She squinted and poked her muzzle forward toward the advancing bears. The black skin of her nose wrinkled and her guard hairs stiffened. "That's not blood of prey but its own blood," Jytte said. "That bear is wounded!"

"If this is a wounded bear, let's help him," Stellan said as he began to gallop toward the bears. He wasn't sure how they could help, but he recalled his mum saying that packing snow onto an open wound was the best way to stop the bleeding.

There were four bears in all — large, full-grown male bears. Only one had been wounded. But like most mature bears, they all bore scars from battles during mating seasons, or from fights over food during the Dying Ice Moons when seals grew sparse.

The dark slashes exposed their black skin where the fur had never grown back.

"Don't fuss, don't fuss. I'm going to be all right, really," the bleeding bear said.

Third and Jytte looked at Stellan, who was staring intently at the strangers. They could tell he was riddling the four bears' minds. Stellan possessed the unique ability to pick up the threads of other creatures' thoughts.

Stellan caught fragmentary glints of the four bears' thinking. *They are wondering if we have seen Roguer bears. If we were captives of the Ice Cap.* "You're rebels, aren't you?" he said, realizing who these bears must be. "You fought against the Timekeepers."

"That we were," replied one bear who had a short black scar across his forehead.

Jytte surveyed the group with awe. These bears had likely fought alongside her father when they stormed the fearsome Ice Cap.

"*Are*, Syril. We are!" the wounded bear corrected him. "We won't give up the fight."

"We thought at first you were Roguers," Jytte said. "But we didn't see the blood banners across your chests."

"They wouldn't wear them here," the bear called Syril said. "But you young'uns watch out. The Roguers have come south and infiltrated this country. One recognized Abbo here." He nodded at the wounded bear. "And attacked."

"Are you from the Nunquivik?" Third asked.

"No, but we are allies with those northern rebels," Syril said.

"Have you ever heard of a bear by the name of Svern?" Jytte asked.

"Svern!" Syril repeated, while the other bears exchanged looks of surprise.

Syril picked up a fistful of snow, pressed it on his bleeding shoulder, then leaned closer to the cubs. "Have you seen him? So you know where he is?"

"No," Jytte said. "We thought you might."

"There've been all sorts of rumors." Syril spoke in a low voice. "Some say he's gone far, far west to beyond the Beyond to gather a regiment of wolves. Then some say that he's dead. There are rumors that they captured him and put him in a black ice hole."

"A black ice hole?" Stellan repeated in a quivering voice.

"Torture site. You see, things have become very bad at the Ice Clock. The Grand Patek has gained vast power. Tell them what you heard, Phynx." He shot a glance at the bear who stood next to him.

"He's gone *yoickhynn*," Phynx whispered. "Out of his mind. It's an owl word."

Jytte felt something curdle in her gut. She almost dared not ask. Finally she said, "Were there any rumors that Svern had gone to the Den of Forever Frost?"

"The Den of Forever Frost?" Phynx repeated, and chuckled to himself. "That's just a legend. I don't believe it's a real place. Or at least, not anymore."

Syril tilted his head, as if reflecting on what Phynx had just said. "I suppose that ancient time now seems so distant to us that it's hard to believe such a place really existed. The bear world has changed so much from the time of Svree. It has become . . . infected by these bears of the Ice Cap. The disease is spreading throughout the kingdoms, from the Nunquivik to the Northern Kingdoms of Ga'Hoole."

Stellan felt something wither inside him. He glanced at his sister. She was blinking and staring at Syril as if trying to digest what he had just said.

"We are sorry." Phynx reached out and touched Jytte on her shoulder. "But why would you think that Svern would go to such a place?"

Stellan tensed. *Don't say it, Jytte! The secret is ours to keep.* The words Stellan could not say aloud reverberated in his own brain with such a clatter that he felt that Jytte might hear them. She did not, of course, but she looked at him with such intensity that he sensed that she knew to stay quiet.

At this point, Jytte's mind was as clear to Stellan as water in a still sea. *One bear's myth*, thought Stellan, *is another's truth.*

"Now, we must go on," Syril said. "But we suggest that you *not* go from where we came. That's where we encountered a *bloodryck*."

"A what?" Third asked.

"A bloodryck. That is the Nunquivik term for the smallest band of Roguers. They are especially thick around good halibut waters. Our mistake!"

"Better to be hungry but live to eat again," Phynx offered cheerfully. "If I were you, I'd swim to the other side — over there where the Firth of Grundensphyrr opens up."

"Grundensphyrr!" Stellan was elated as he heard the word. "That's the firth our mum came from."

"It's not a far piece from here. Go into the Bay of Fangs. Halfway up, you take a port turn and you shall be in the Firth of Grundensphyrr. There might be some fish up there. Not halibut, but smaller stuff. Nothing to attract Roguers."

The cubs and the four rebel bears said good-bye. As the cubs trudged to the edge of the icy shore and slipped into the water, Jytte muttered, "The Den of Forever Frost is not just a legend. It's real, and we're going to find it."

CHAPTER 4

The Ruminations of Cleve

Cleve dipped out of the cloudbank. His progress was slower than he had anticipated, as a headwind had kicked up. His mind was consumed with the three cubs he had seen and heard. He felt a coldness creep through him, as if a shadow had seeped into that most delicate of all owl organs — his gizzard. The gizzard was where owls felt their deepest and most powerful feelings. The bears appeared innocent enough. They were, after all, just cubs, second years most likely. In the fragments of conversation he had picked up, he discovered that two of them spoke a bit of Krakish, for their vocabulary was flecked with several random words of that language, but with the slight twang of the Nunquivik. Odd accent, the burr of Krakish mingled with that twang.

No one knew what went on in the Nunquivik. For years the bears of the Northern Kingdom had avoided any contact with the Nunquivik. But as the sealing became worse, particularly up near the Hrath'gar region, several bears had found their way across the Nunqua Sea to that sparsely populated land. And then odd events ensued, events that Cleve thought of as a trail of blood. Creatures began appearing — motherless cubs who had suffered severe wounds. An odd species of seal not normally seen in the Everwinter Sea became more prevalent. Their pelts, which had a peculiar bluish tinge, were lacerated. Many of these creatures died before Cleve and his chaw of medics could help them. The few who survived spoke gibberish.

And this business about the Den of Forever Frost? He had a dim recollection of hearing about it. It was part of the myth of the Northern Kingdoms. But it was very difficult to sort out myth from actual history. His mate, Otulissa, was a scholar. She often cautioned about confusing myth with history. She called it mythstory. But then she would always add, "Many myths, however, do have their origins in history. But one must know history to begin to understand mythstory."

Cleve was not such a scholar. He was a healer. He had helped many of those wounded creatures who had arrived from the Nunquivik. He had been a medic on the battlefield during the owl wars in days past but never a warrior himself. He was a gizzard resistor. Otulissa was a warrior. Had two more opposite owls ever been attracted to each other? The owls of the Great Ga'Hoole Tree often wondered. And even though Otulissa had been gravely wounded some years before and was no longer able to serve in combat, she remained a superb military strategist.

Cleve was now on his way back to the Great Ga'Hoole Tree, flying through the straits of the Ice Narrows that connected the Everwinter Sea with the Sea of Hoolemere. Scores of puffins, simpleminded, brightly colored birds, had lined up on the cliffs to wave at him. He tilted his wings back and forth. They cheered. "We love a parade!" one squawked. *One owl does not a parade make*, thought Cleve. There was no teaching puffins, however.

It was a flawless day. This often happened after severe weather such as the storm that had swept through. The sky was cloudless and intensely blue. There was no wind, so the sea, now almost thawed, was green as the leaves in the Silverveil, the lushest of all the territories in Ga'Hoole. This was a benign world, a world apart in many ways. Peace had reigned for several years now in Ga'Hoole. The last war had been the War of the Ember. A young king had died in that war. Great Glaux, the owl kingdoms deserved these years of peace!

If something evil was happening with the great white bears of the Nunquivik, what business was it of theirs? The Nunquivik was a far-off land. It was bear business, not owl business. And yet he could see those cubs were frightened. Orphaned and frightened. And what was this Den of Forever Frost? There had been too many bears plying these waters of the Everwinter Sea and its firths of late, and too many bloody trails.

Cleve flew on until he was over the Great Ga'Hoole Tree then he began to descend — not to the usual landing limb that served owls coming from the north, but the large limb to the south and west corner where he knew he would find his mate, Otulissa. Since she had put aside her battle claws and war hammer, Otulissa devoted herself primarily to the cultivation of the hanging gardens in the lower part of the tree canopy. A variety of mosses flourished and dozens of air plants floated from vines. With their multicolored blossoms and delicate fragrances that wafted on the breeze, the hanging gardens were a kind of *glaumora*, the owl word for heaven. A glaumora on earth.

As so often when he approached, his mate's back was turned to him, as she was cultivating some new little seedlings she had just discovered. Otulissa used a drip stem to feed them a mild solution of water mixed with the nutritious sap that oozed from certain branches of the tree during the season of the Copper Rose. Cleve and Otulissa had not been blessed with hatchlings, but Otulissa was not one to languish with regrets of any kind. The tenderness she would have lavished on owl chicks she poured into her plants. Without turning around, she said, "I think you've got a burr in your starboard fringe feathers, dear. I could hear you a quarter league away."

"Oh my!" Cleve sighed. Her wing had been damaged in the infamous battle with the blue owls, but she had recovered her flight skills over time. Although she did fly a tad clumsily in the winter during the furling winds, when drafts rolled under one like waves on a raucous sea.

"Any reports from the blackcaps?"

"Unfortunately, yes," Otulissa sighed.

"More dead cubs?"

"No, thankfully . . ."

"Then what is it, Otulissa?"

"Apparently there are signs of movement on the southeast coast of the Nunqua Sea. Tracks, you know."

"Oh yes. I came upon some cubs there. But they were fine. No wounds."

"Not cubs' tracks, Cleve. Bears, immense bears from the far north. They grow them larger there, apparently. Gigantic bears, the blackcaps reported. A cub could fit into one of their tracks! You know the rumors about those bears from Nunquivik. They're strange. Strange and violent."

"Are any of the blackcaps here now?"

"Yes. I think they were going into the dining hollow for a bit of nourishment. They're quite exhausted, so don't wear them out, Cleve."

❧

The dining hall was quiet. It would be a while before the owls gathered for tweener, their first meal of the day before evening flight. Only one nest-maid was serving as the table. It was a custom at the Great Tree that the nest-maid snakes provided not just nest-keeping skills but functioned as tables in the dining hall. They tended to be long and plump. Partly coiled, this one was stretched out to only half her length, as the blackcaps, a species of warblers, were so tiny in comparison to most owls that they hardly took up any room at a snake table. The warblers did look exhausted and picked at their food.

"Poor little things. Hardly have eaten a speck. Cook soft-boiled just one caterpillar for all six of them," a nest-maid fretted.

"Now, Mrs. M., don't be anxious," Cleve replied. "Their digestive tracts can't handle too much after their long flights."

"Yes, Mrs. Miniver. Take no offense," said Maisie, a female and the captain of the warbler troop, known as a glee, in a small squeaky voice. They were known as blackcaps, but only the males had black feathers on their heads. They all, however, had bright orange legs.

Maisie continued. "Don't worry; by our next flight we'll be up to a whole caterpillar apiece."

Indeed, these high-speed minuscule fliers who crossed vast oceans doubled their body weight before their long migrations.

"Oh yes," a male replied. "And we love the hot sauce. But a bit too spicy on an empty tummy."

Cleve came up to the snake table where they perched, or barely perched, for their legs seemed unsteady.

"I understand you were debriefed in the parliament hollow already. You detected some bear movement, am I correct?"

"Indeed, sir. We don't quite understand it. Many cubs coming from the north. Some wounded. It appears they might be being chased. But some larger bears also wounded. Don't know quite what to make of it."

"Yes, troubling. But I just want to thank you personally for your service."

"No need, sir. T'was an honor to serve," Maisie replied. A bit of caterpillar hung from her beak. "But things are not good, sir, not good," she murmured ominously.

CHAPTER 5

Darkness Beckons

It had been three days, three hours, forty-two minutes, thirty-seven seconds, and two milliseconds since the old Chronos had fallen from the highest parapet of the Ice Clock. Svenna could now calculate instantly the passages of time down to the single millisecond. In this sense, she had become one of them, a perfect numerator for the infernal Ice Clock and its worshippers. But she was no worshipper — she was an infidel. The rage of a heretic smoldered within her. And there was nothing as wrathful as a mother taken from her cubs. She had had no choice when the Roguers came. She wouldn't have let anyone take her cubs, though she would've been even more terrified had she known the truth: They devoured cubs at the Ice Cap. The poor creatures, known as Tick Tocks, were sacrificed to the clock, torn apart on the escapement wheel.

And yet she was expected to work with a small replica of the clock as she calculated the arc swing of its pendulum. For a faithless and questioning Timekeeper, Svenna had advanced rapidly to work as a personal assistant to the Mystress of the Chimes, where she labored on endless calculations.

But even just peering at the pendulum forced her to imagine the diabolical wheel. She began her calculations but felt her stomach churning as she imagined this horrendous instrument of torture. How could they call it a god? How could it be worshipped?

She had only glimpsed one Tick Tock up close. She'd been in ice lock for a code violation. To be precise, violation number 106 of the Complication Code. She had asked *why* they were doing these endless calculations. What exactly was the purpose of the clock? To ask such questions was strictly forbidden. While in her cell, a Tick Tock had appeared — a strange, ghostly little cub. He was maimed, of course, missing a paw but not bleeding. His name was Juuls.

She tried her best to banish these bloody thoughts from her head as she pursued the tedious work. She scratched out the figures with a sharp sliver of fish bone on a tablet of sealscap, dipping the point into a small pot of squid ink. The figures and mathematical symbols floated before her eyes but connected to nothing — they'd mean nothing to a true bear.

And once upon a time, she had been a true bear. She had given birth to cubs. Nursed them, begun to teach them the ways of ice. And what did she do now? Nothing. She, the largest predator on earth, was a slave to these little figures she scratched out on the sealscap.

The work was endless. In addition to her timekeeping duties in the harmonics lab, Svenna served as an ice char to keep the living quarters of the Mystress spotless.

The Mystress of the Chimes was an odd sort of bear. With her dazzling white coat, she was as vain as she was beautiful. She imported willow twigs as part of her beauty treatment, claiming they made her fur whiter, and that its blinding whiteness made other bears' pelts sallow in comparison. There were rumors that she also used the blood of young seals to keep her coat lustrous. Tending to her was exhausting work, as the Mystress was an exacting bear.

Fastidious about her den, the Mystress did not tolerate any grit on the ice floor. She claimed it disturbed her footpads. In her sleeping den she had arranged her bedding so that it faced north. She was quite insistent about this. The snow for the bed must be plumped and of softest flakes.

The lab was in the Mystress's extensive ice den, which had several connected smaller dens. Some were for receiving guests, others for studying and sleeping. The Mystress's first name was Galilya, but of course, Svenna was forbidden to address her in such a personal manner. It would be a violation. She must always use the term *Mystress* when speaking to her.

Svenna had completed the calculations and had begun scraping the ice floor in the receiving den when she heard the Mystress's sharp voice.

"Great Ursus, the Stellata Council meets in ten minutes, fourteen seconds, and three milliseconds," she said, rushing in from the harmonics lab. "It's high council. Quickly, Svenna. My jewels, are they polished?"

"Certainly, Mystress."

"Bring them to me and help with the latching."

"Right away, Mystress."

The Mystress's rank demanded that she wear her coronet, a headband studded with emeralds and diamonds, to meetings in the Stellata Chamber. She was also required to wear the special sash that had the emblems of the Holy Order of the Gilraan, the highest level of Timekeepers. Svenna brought these to her and helped the Mystress arrange the sash on an angle across her chest.

"I'll do the coronet myself."

There was a full-length isinglass mirror in her dressing chamber that the Mystress stepped in front of as she affixed the coronet to the top of her head.

"Earrings!" she snapped, holding out a paw. Svenna handed her the two diamonds that resembled the shape of the clock's pendulum. Galilya, the Mystress of the Chimes, then took a step back. Regarding herself in the mirror, she squinted.

"Stunning!" she declared. The reflection spoke into the nothingness between the mirror and the Mystress. She turned to Svenna. "And I have a new set of harmonics calcs for you to work on." She thrust out a paw with the sealscap. "Have them completed by the time I'm back," she snapped.

⚬⚬

Svenna returned to the harmonics lab and sighed as she began this new set of calculations. Svenna hated the work. It was so unbearlike. She hardly knew anymore what it meant to be a bear. She no longer had to hunt, as food was "served" here at the Ice Clock. She had no cubs to look after and teach. There were no stories to tell. The only "stories" were these inexhaustible equations that numerators such as herself worked on endlessly.

Svenna sat for several minutes and simply stared at the wall. She felt if she performed another calculation, the essential bear part of her being might just slip away into the tiny numbers and mathematical symbols that were scattered across the sealscap. *My life is meaningless. What is my life without my cubs? Why should I go on?* It was as if a splinter of ice had lodged in her heart. And if she thought of her cubs too much, a terror would begin to invade her. A wobbliness took over her body; her very bones shuddered and felt unstrung. The cubs' adorable little faces would float through her mind's eye and then dissolve into nothingness. The feeling of their soft furry bodies that had nestled into hers would begin to melt away. She had to train herself not to think about the cubs from whom she was separated before they could be properly named, for one did not name cubs until they were well into their second year. Yet she had no choice but to continue — she had to fight and survive long enough to return to them.

So many times a day tears began to well up in Svenna's eyes, as they did now when she began her work on checking this set of calcs that the Mystress had demanded. She was almost fearful to turn her head toward the figures that awaited her attention.

In addition to her own cubs, she worried about the little Tick Tock cub Juuls. She had to escape the Ice Cap as soon as possible but hoped she'd be able to help the Tick Tocks in some way before she left.

As she peered at the wall by the ice table where she was set to work, she noticed a fine crack in the ice. She squinted so she might see it better and felt something stir inside her. She looked about to make sure that no one was watching. She then rose from the bench where she had been working and, hardly daring to breathe, moved toward the crack. There was another crack, and then another.

There were four cracks in all. Not natural cracks. Ice never cracked so precisely. It looked as if a perfect square had been incised on the ice wall. Wiping the tears from her eyes, she brought her face close to the cracks. She began to trace them with her claw. She heard a slight creak. She drew back her head suddenly in alarm. A panel was opening. A slot of darkness became visible. It beckoned her. Her heart was thumping wildly in her chest. As the slot became wider, she could not resist but step through and into the tunnel. Cautiously she began to walk a few steps, then more. The path dipped a bit, and when she had walked a fair number of steps, she suddenly heard the scrape of a whispery voice in the darkness. Svenna jerked about and saw a small fleeting, shadowless figure disappear down another ice corridor.

"Juuls? Juuls! Come back!" It was the little ghostly cub, one of the cubs that had been maimed on the escapement wheel. She now realized that this cub did not simply seem ghostly but was a ghost — a *gillygaskin*. But if it had died, why had it not gone to Ursulana, where the spirits of dead bears always ascended by climbing the star ladder? This was a cursed place indeed.

CHAPTER 6

The So-Called Legends

The three cubs felt a change in the current as they swam into the Bay of Fangs. The bay was wide with tall trees that fringed the shores, the tallest the cubs had ever seen. A slight wind stirred their branches, producing an odd murmuring sound they had never heard before.

"It's as if the trees are talking," Third said.

"Not exactly talking. Maybe just whispering to the wind." Stellan cocked his head.

"Imagine trees whispering to one another. What might they be saying?" Third mused.

"Maybe they're saying, 'You're here, cubs,'" Jytte replied. "'You're here in the land of your mum and your da.'"

"Or," Stellan added, "maybe they're calling to an owl."

"Perfect for owls!" Jytte exclaimed. "I'd love to see one of their dens."

"Not dens," Stellan corrected her. "Hollows. That's what owls call their dens. Hard to imagine being so small you could live in a tree hole."

"Nice view, though," Third said.

There were several firths that cut from the bay into the shore, but the current was against them and it took them the better part of the afternoon to reach the halfway point in the very long bay.

"I think I see it — the Firth of Grundensphyrr. Remember the map Skagen showed us? That was Mum's firth," Jytte called back to Stellan and Third. She felt excitement course through her at the idea of being close to the firth where their mum was born and reared. And possibly close to the venerable and storied Den of Forever Frost.

Stellan hesitated. So often Jytte's imagination got the better of her, and then only disappointment followed. "Now, remember, Jytte," he said carefully. "Only one of the firths connects directly to the Den of Forever Frost. And Skagen himself did not know which one. We might have to do a bit of exploring before we find the right one."

"Yes, Stellan, I remember," Jytte said wearily. "But also remember that he believed it was in a firth connected possibly to either Mum or Da."

"You're right. Yes, of course," Stellan said quickly. It was a difficult balance he had to keep with Jytte. He had to support her but not encourage her too much. Nevertheless, as they came around a bend, the coast began to look more and more like the maps they had studied in Skagen's den.

"I think we might be in the Firth of Grundensphyrr!" Stellan exclaimed. "Just think of it, Jytte; this water touched our mum's pelt. Maybe the stories she told us came from here!"

"This *is* a place of stories!" Jytte said. "I'm sure of it."

"How do you mean?" Third asked.

"There were owls that came here too," Jytte said. "Remember, Stellan, Mum told us about the owls called skogs. They were the storytelling owls, and when Mum was little, she used to swim up quietly and listen sometimes. That's where she first heard the tale of Svenka, our great-great-oh-so-many-times-great-grandmother who helped the noble owl queen Siv."

"They even say," Stellan added, "that at the Great Ga'Hoole Tree there is an ancient portrait of Svenka honoring her for defending Queen Siv, the spotted owl of the Northern Kingdoms."

Third was envious of the two cubs. Whereas they longed to be as close to their mum as possible, a chill passed through Third's bones whenever he thought of his mother, Taaka.

"Look over there," Jytte said. Not far away, several bears were climbing out of the water onto a rocky spit of land.

"More rebels?" Third asked.

"I don't think so," Stellan said, looking over his shoulder. "See just behind us? That's a family coming down the beach." A mother bear and two cubs sped by as Jytte, Stellan, and Third climbed out of the water.

"Hold on, Jakey!" the mum called out. "There's time."

"I want to be first, Mum!"

The mother looked at Stellan and rolled her eyes. "He wants to be first. What else is new?"

Jytte stared at the bear suspiciously. Where had these bears come from? The Nunquivik? "Where are you going?" Jytte asked.

The bear seemed surprised. "The Firth of Grundensphyrr, of course!"

Jytte and Stellan exchanged excited looks. The Firth of Grundensphyrr was on Skagen's map. They were on the right path again.

"Little Jakey is *not* going to be first," Jytte whispered to Third. "Watch me." She bounded ahead.

CHAPTER 7

A Strange Device

There were at least ten other bears already assembled on the spit. The ice had almost melted entirely from this piece of land, and small flowers with purple blossoms sprang from the earth.

Jytte went up to a female bear, Jakey's mum. "Pardon me, can I ask what you and all these bears are doing here?"

"Oh, it's a historic region, my dear. We live to the west, but we've always wanted to come here. They've just recently opened up one of the caves to visitors. It played an important role during the War of the Ice Talons."

Jytte and Stellan exchanged glances. *There might be important information about the Den of Forever Frost here*, Jytte thought.

Stellan was uncertain, but he knew from the expression on Jytte's face there would be no stopping her now. They fell into the group and followed.

"Ooooh! Look at those," Jytte said, gesturing toward the purple blossoms. She had a dim recollection of their mum telling them about flowers, but she'd never seen a real one. "What are they?"

"Ice violets," Jakey's mother said. "First sign of spring here."

Stellan was about to say that there were no flowers in the Nunquivik but decided not to. Best if no one knew where they came from.

The ground felt good under their feet. *The snow melts almost completely here!* Third marveled. He noticed Jytte and Stellan scratching at the ground with their claws.

"No wonder odd things grow here." Jytte's voice was filled with wonder as she examined the soil. "It's as if the earth feeds them."

Stellan's attention was caught by a bright, tiny orange flower quivering in the breeze like a small flame. He realized how very few colors there had been in the Nunquivik, except of course when the night sky was radiant and pulsing with the hues of the *ahalikki*. With every step this new land became more magical.

Up ahead, Jakey and his mother had stopped alongside several other bears. As the cubs approached, one of the bears — a female — stepped forward. She was tall and rather gaunt. Her eyes had a pinched look, as if she were squinting to bring something into sharper focus. There was unnerving glint in her eyes, and when her gaze settled on Jytte, Stellan took a step closer to his sister and tried to casually rest a paw on her shoulder, but

Jytte shook it off. *Don't baby me!* Stellan picked up the thought as clearly as if she had barked at him.

"Welcome to the Firth of Grundensphyrr, bears." She nodded at them all now. "My name is Grynda. Today, I'll be guiding you through one of the most historically significant sites in the entire Northern Kingdoms.

"I am a certified member of the Decency Order of Bear History and Genealogy. I come from one of the oldest and most revered of the bear families, the clan of Svelynk. As you all know, there are eighteen bear clans, or there were at one time. Each clan's name derived from one of the eighteen major stars that comprise the constellation of the Great Bear. My clan's star was way up the spine of the bear, the backbone," she said with a small note of triumph.

Stellan bristled slightly. Their mum said only vulgar bears bragged about ancestors. He hoped that Jytte wouldn't start trying to brag about their own ancestors, Svree and the Great Marven and Svenka.

Jytte sidled up to her brother. "Why do we need a guide? Can't we just explore on our own?"

"I don't think they want us to be on our own," Third said warily.

"They? Who's 'they'?" Jytte narrowed her eyes.

"Well," Stellan said, "that's the problem. I feel there is something bigger going on here than just a history lesson."

"So here we are on the banks of the legendary Firth of Grundensphyrr," Grynda explained. "One of the most popular tourist destinations in these kingdoms, a storied place. The place where the bears and the owls of Ga'Hoole came together as allies in the ancient owl wars against forces of evil. But many of the tales you've heard are just that — stories and not actual history. Stories are not facts. They are alternate non-information, perhaps misinformation, with no value except for mild entertainment. We in the Decency Order find it profoundly offensive when myth is confused with actual history. Indeed, false stories can offend and corrupt our faith — our *vrahkyn*, the old Krakish word for faith. So it is our mission to untangle those knots of misleading, fanciful tales and give you the true history and restore the faith, the vrahkyn."

Jytte and Stellan exchanged a startled look. Their mother had said that stories restore belief and their truths can change the world. Some of the other bears nodded as if they understood, but many looked rather mystified.

"So on our tour," Grynda continued, "you will learn a new kind of truth."

Does truth change over time? Stellan wondered.

Jytte raised her paw and Grynda frowned. "I prefer that you save the questions until the end of the tour."

"You just said they never happened, these legends." Jytte struggled to make her voice forceful but still polite. The polite part was hard. Her heart was thumping in her chest.

"Correct. These stories never happened."

"And that they damaged our faith . . . our vrahkyn?" Jytte asked.

"Indeed!" A brittle light flashed in Grynda's eyes.

"How . . . how do you discover if our faith is damaged?" Jytte stammered a bit.

"I was about to get to that," Grynda replied. Now the light was gone. Jytte cocked her head and looked straight into Grynda's black eyes. They were like tiny holes. They reflected nothing. It was the nothingness that disturbed Jytte. This was a hollow bear. "If you will follow me into the cave just ahead, I shall show you a marvelous device."

At that moment a female warbler swooped from the sky and skimmed the crown of Grynda's head. "Ah, the migration of warblers this time of year. It's called the Warbler Moon here in the Northern Kingdoms of Ga'Hoole." She tipped her head up toward the sky.

A young bear, perhaps just a season younger than Jytte and Stellan, had raised her paw to ask a question. She seemed to be alone.

"Another question," sniffed Grynda. "So many questions and we've hardly started."

"Just to say, madam bear —"

"I am a prefect. That is what bears of instruction of the Decency Order are called."

"Actually, it's not a question, prefect," the young cub said.

"Ah, now who's the prefect? You came to correct me, I suppose."

"No, no, prefect, but I just know that in these parts the owls call this moon the Moon of the Golden Rain, not the Warbler Moon."

"Thank you for that information. Would you prefer to be the prefect and continue the lecture? You seem to be an authority."

"Never, madam!" Stellan felt anger boiling in the young cub's head.

"So as I was saying, there was never any truth to such legends."

Jytte slid closer to the young bear. "Do you believe her?" she whispered.

"She is half right. The legends that began here were mostly those from the old times of the owls. But it was here that the owls and the bears first came together in the time of the ancient wars, sometimes called the Hag Wars, in the time before Lyze of Kiel."

"How do you know all this?" Stellan whispered. "You look so young."

"I was born just two Halibut Moons past."

"Like us," Jytte said, gesturing toward Stellan.

"Yes, but not exactly."

"How do you mean not exactly?" Third asked. Beneath the fluffy white facial fur, Third noticed a deep crease in the bear's forehead, similar to that of an elderly male bear. Yet this bear was female and too young to have such a crease even if she were male. Was there also a tracery of fighting scars?

"I'm an old soul," the bear replied. *Perhaps this bear walks back through time as I walk through dreams*, Third thought.

"Now." The strident voice of the bear Grynda rasped the air. "If you follow me to those cliffs straight ahead, we shall enter the foyer of the ceremonial hall where the bears from yesteryear gathered to hear the false stories around the time of the Great Melting." She paused dramatically. "And I shall show you the amazing device that we call the Vrahkynyx, which tests one's faith."

Something in Grynda's tone made Stellan shudder, but it was too late to turn around. He felt as if there were other eyes watching them. The "they" he had imagined before. Were there in fact guards here? Why would there be guards?

He suddenly felt vulnerable. He was reluctant to be left with this guide despite the fact that there were other bears around them waiting to enter the ceremonial hall.

"It's all right, Stellan," Jytte whispered, trying to sound unruffled. "Let's keep moving."

Third put out a paw to stop her. "I'm not so sure, Jytte. I'm having odd feelings."

"Me too," Stellan said. Something was not quite right about Grynda. There was something so unbearish about her. He couldn't imagine her hunting, or rearing cubs and teaching them to hunt, or swimming, or digging out a den on the pack ice.

"I can't explain what it is. Almost a smell." Third's shiny black nose began to quiver. He looked about as if some hidden shadow, a shadow from one of his terrible dreams, was stalking him.

"I don't care," Jytte said. "She might still have important information about the Den of Forever Frost. We have to keep going."

The cubs followed Grynda along with the others into a large cave. As they walked, they noticed enormous outcroppings of rock and ice projecting from the walls.

"It was here," Grynda continued, "when the seas rose during the time of the Great Melting, that the Great Marven stories were told. Though, of course, the Great Marven never existed. He was merely a myth, a figment of some bear's silly imagination." A gasp swept through the space, and Stellan felt something crumble inside himself. The Marven stories his mum had told them always gave him hope. Swimming had not come as easily to him as it had to Jytte. But Marven too was said to have a slight twist to his rear paw. It was a twist perhaps just like his own, and yet Marven had become a great swimmer.

"Is Marven just a myth?" a somewhat elderly bear with a stooped appearance asked, his voice full of doubt. "I've heard these stories of the Great Marven all my life."

"I'll tell you exactly how it came to be," Grynda replied confidently. "The bear who told those stories was indeed a wonderful storyteller but a terrible swimmer himself. The truth was that Marven could not swim at all. Not one bit. He was deformed and a beggar."

Stellan looked down at the twist in his own hind foot, and something began to shrivel inside him. He felt Jytte reach for his paw as if to assure him that the stories of Marven were real. Yet this bear Grynda had called him a beggar, a thief, and a liar. Was this the truth that she said the tour would reveal?

"Now onto the Vrahkynyx. Right this way, please." Grynda led them down a winding passage to a niche in the wall where she stopped.

"Stand back, please, while I uncover this amazing device."

With a flourish she snatched a seal skin that was covering the niche to reveal an odd instrument. "Is it not a thing of beauty — of beauty, truth, and faith?"

The three cubs froze as their eyes traveled over the strange apparatus. A sickening feeling began to well up in each of them. The structure was made of metal and odd pieces — pieces they had seen before. This was, in fact, a timepiece that had been taken apart and reassembled into something just as frightening as the great Ice Clock.

"How does this work?" Stellan asked nervously.

"It fits on your head. I then ask you some questions, and the dials on the Vrahkynyx can read your faith. But even if you register as having a low level of faith, we can help you."

Faith in what? thought Stellan. And then he plucked the thought right out of Grynda's twisted mind. *Faith in the clock. The Great Ice Clock of the Ice Cap.*

"We've got to get out of here!" Stellan whispered. He wheeled about and glared at Jytte. "Follow me now."

"Where are you going?" called the bear Grynda. "That is not authorized. You cannot just leave."

Frantically, the cubs began to scramble out of the cave just as guards suddenly appeared behind Grynda. "Go!" Stellan shouted to Jytte and Third as they took off. These weren't guards, he realized.

They were Roguers from the Ice Cap.

CHAPTER 8

"You Are Not Made of Lies"

The cubs shot from the cave and continued running at a hard pace until they found themselves on a high cliff that hung over the firth. They skidded to a halt and looked down into the dark waters below. Their claws gripped the edge. Behind them they could hear the shouts of the Roguer bears growing closer. The thunder of their paws shook the ground.

"Oh, Great Ursus!" Stellan gasped. "There's no choice. We have to jump." He grasped each cub's paw. "One — two — three!" he cried, then launched himself into the air. Their eyes were squeezed shut, their paws held fast. Down, down, down, and then a splash.

When the three cubs surfaced, they were sputtering but still holding one another's paws.

"Now swim!" Stellan shouted. He thought of Marven and his twisted paw and swam as hard as he could. The current was with them, and they reached the other side of the firth faster than he'd thought possible. Staggering onto the beach, they looked back. There were no bears on the other side. The Roguers must have stopped at the cliff, not believing that the cubs would ever jump.

"We walked right into a death trap!" Jytte said.

"There must be Roguers all over this place," Third said raggedly as he gasped for breath. "They've invaded. The bears of the Ice Clock are here!"

"Where will we be safe?" Jytte asked.

"Maybe nowhere," Third said dismally. "But we can be careful."

"It looks like there's an old den in the bank just ahead. Must have been left from this past winter," Stellan said. "We could use it, but we need to camouflage it."

Cautiously the cubs approached the opening of the den.

Third peered inside. "It's abandoned, so we're not taking anybody's den."

"It smells like skunk bear," Stellan said. His nose wrinkled, and there was a touch of doom in his voice.

Jytte and Stellan had been attacked by a skunk bear in the Nunquivik. Jytte would never forget her terror when the creature seized her and wrapped her in a death crush. Somehow, Stellan had managed to leap onto the skunk bear's back and scratch its face. The creature dropped Jytte immediately and was left writhing in a pool of its own blood.

With those memories still vivid in their minds, the cubs

cautiously entered the den. Stellan looked around, relieved. "This skunk bear hasn't been here in a long time."

"Are you sure, Stellan?" Third asked nervously.

"Look at these bones." The bones of the skunk bear's prey were scattered around, but they were bleached white and brittle. Whoever had pulled off the meat had done so long ago.

"Stellan's right," Jytte said. "Remember how Skagen camouflaged his cave? Let's take some branches from those trees and gather some of those dead limbs on the ground."

Stellan and Third nodded solemnly. What hadn't they learned from Skagen? Every bit of knowledge he'd shared about the stars, all the stories he'd told of his homeland in the Schrynn Gar, were like a radiant gems from some secret cache. "Imagine this," he would often begin. "Imagine how long it takes that light from the Svree star to reach the earth. Hundreds, maybe thousands of light-years."

As the cubs worked together to conceal the entrance to the skunk bear's cave, they fell quiet — overwhelmed by their memories of Skagen and of their recent terrifying escape from the firth.

Finally Jytte broke the silence. "You don't believe what that awful Grynda said about the stories, right?"

"No, not really . . . ," Stellan said. "But what if —?"

"Listen to me, cubs!" Third cut in sharply. "Forget everything that awful bear said. You are not made of lies. When creatures tell you not to believe something, you have to ask why. What are they fearful of you discovering?"

"What do you think?" Stellan asked. "What's Grynda afraid of?"

"I'm going to have to sleep on that," Third replied. Stellan and Jytte looked at each other knowingly. It was a strange territory that the little cub wandered through when he slept and went on his dream walks.

"I'm not sleepy in the least," Jytte said, admiring their handiwork with the branches.

"Then don't sleep," Third said as he lowered himself to the ground and placed his head on his paws. "Tell your stories and mend your doubts and so mend yourselves. And then we'll go on. We'll do what Skagen told us. We'll find your father. He'll take us to the Den of Forever Frost. Now tell your stories. They are not lies. They will strengthen you."

CHAPTER 9

The Yarner of Yore

It was the season halfway between two moons — the Moon of the First Cracks and the Dying Ice Moons — so the cubs' stories were accompanied by the plinking sounds of melting ice, as well as the creaks and fracturing of ice out in the open waters.

In the skunk bear's cave, Third had fallen asleep halfway through the story of the Great Marven and gone dreamwalking. In the past, he had always walked through the fragments of other bears' dreams, like those of his treacherous mother, Taaka. But this dream walk was different. At first, he thought he was following the misty tracks of the frog Sylvia — he saw a small creature springing from one floe to another and detected the new beats of a freshly melting heart. But those heartbeats were too powerful to belong to a little frog. Indeed, the rhythms seemed much more like those of a . . . bear?

The dream that Third walked through was adrift with ice fragments. He skipped from one to another, trying to close in on the misty figure ahead.

Unlike previous dream walks, this one did not frighten Third. He had no desire to turn back but instead felt a strong, almost overpowering urge to catch up with the mysterious creature. The fragments of ice were coalescing as if there had been a sudden acceleration of seasons.

And yet the light did not disappear as it did in the winter moons. Third seemed to be in a bright yet sunless place that glared with a spikey geometry of frost. There were a million points of dazzling light. The path was solid underfoot, and as Third began to wind his way through a network of tunnels, he realized he was following the shadow of a somewhat familiar bear, perhaps near his own age.

The bear stopped in front of an ice figure of a much larger bear, then turned around to look at Third. Something odd began to occur. Third sensed another presence. It was as if the spirit of that ice bear had suddenly become two, and one was that of an old soul. Or were they actually the same bear?

"You are the same —" Third started to say. But by this time, the smaller bear had been completely absorbed by the larger bear, who lifted a paw to his mouth as if to hush Third.

"As I said, I am an old soul."

Third was mystified. How many bears could one single bear contain?

"But I thought you were a female and born of the Halibut Moon."

"I am all those. Born through every moon."

Every moon? Third thought. That seemed impossible. But then he thought of the wood frog Sylvia, who could die and then die again and again.

"And what is your name?" Third asked.

"Eervs."

"Eervs? I've never heard such a name."

"There is much you've never heard, young'un, or seen."

Third tipped his head and peered at the bear, more confused than ever. "But you were a cub when I first met you. That's what I don't understand."

Eervs sighed deeply. "I have to live many lives for my work."

"But what is your work?"

"I find lost souls."

"You mean dead creatures?"

"Not dead. Creatures once brave who have lost their way. They are like lost legends, and they walk in a never-ending mist. That is the meaning of my name, Eervs — finder, restorer."

"What lost legends?"

"Look around you. Look around."

Third began to swivel his head. This bright and icy place seemed to dissolve. A vaguely familiar landscape began to melt out of the now dim light. Beneath his feet, there was a wrinkle. *Am I standing on a map?* he wondered. Indeed, it looked just like a map Skagen had showed them. He was actually straddling an island. He recognized the shape. It was Stormfast, across from a firth called Uthermere.

"Go!" Eervs said forcefully. "They will know. A wolf shall dwell with the seal, a toothwalker shall lie down with a fox, and cubs shall lead the way."

Go — but where should he go? He was lost in a maze of dreams, of multiple images. He did not know which way to turn. He wanted to wake up. "Cubs," Third whispered hoarsely in his dream.

CHAPTER 10

A Parliament of Owls

An emergency meeting had been called in the parliament hollow of the Great Tree. A dozen owls of varying species, ranging from tiny pygmy owls to snowies, perched on the curved white branch of a birch tree. In the center of the parliament, the now elderly king, Soren, was settled on a gnarled branch encrusted with lichen and swagged in moss. When Soren had become king, he had dispensed with the massive stump that had once served as the throne for the previous monarchs of the Great Tree. He had never been comfortable perched on the lofty stump. He preferred to be closer to the members of the parliament, and most important, at eye level. The gnarled branch that projected from a wall allowed him to come much closer to the tiny bird that trembled on another slender branch known as the *wykensprat*, which in the Hoolian language translated to witness stand. The witness in this case was an errant warbler, Carrick, a young female who had been blown off course.

"Carrick," Soren said softly. "And what does it mean?"

"Rock, sir, literally."

"Very unusual name for a bird."

"Warblers, sir, often have unusual names."

"I see, but you said literally that was the meaning. Is there another meaning to your name?"

"Yes, sir. Steady. Enduring."

"Ah, like the qualities of rock." The tiny warbler swayed a bit. She did not in this moment feel steady at all.

Otulissa raised a talon to speak.

"Yes, Otulissa?"

"I feel, Soren — I mean, sir —"

"Soren is fine, old friend."

"Well, I feel, Soren, that young Carrick here is quite exhausted, and it would be wise to let her speak quickly and tell us what she witnessed in the Firth of Grundensphyrr."

"Of course. Continue, Carrick."

"Yes . . . uh . . . as the spotted owl said, I happened to be flying over."

"You are a free flyer and not a member of a glee. Am I correct?" Soren asked.

"*Fyre spiritu*," Otulissa murmured.

"What's that, Otulissa?" Soren asked.

"Fyre spiritu — that's Warblese for free flyer."

"Ah, yes, of course," Soren said. Then he turned to Carrick. "Otulissa is our tree scholar, and a linguist as well. She has mastered several languages. Now continue with your story."

"As I was saying, I was flying over the southeastern point that projects into the firth. I noticed a gathering of bears."

"That in itself is unusual," Soren said. "They are known to be most solitary creatures."

"Yes, sir. But these were gathered. It was a low ceiling. The clouds were arguing, as we warblers say. I was afforded good camouflage and therefore I could listen in. A sudden downdraft plummeted me quite close to the speaker — a female bear of medium size who had introduced herself to the bears as Grynda."

Soren cast his eyes toward his daughter, Blythe, who was now his first lieutenant.

"Could these bears be the same ones the blackcaps were tracking?"

"No, sir, they were still far to the north and had not yet entered the channel waters between the Nunquivik and Everwinter Sea. With the adverse winds, they were slowed down quite a bit."

Soren turned back to Carrick. "So what did you hear in the downdraft?"

The warbler cleared her tiny throat a bit and then began to speak.

"The bear's exact words were this: 'Welcome! Welcome to the legendary Firth of Grundensphyrr, one of the most popular tourist destinations in the Northern Kingdoms, a storied place. But it is just that — stories, not actual history. We of the Decency Order find it profoundly offensive when myth or legend is confused with actual history. So it is our mission as members of the Decency Order of bear history to untangle that knot of misleading fanciful tales and give you the true history.'"

"Decency!" Soren gasped, and Otulissa's beak fell open, as did many of the old timers'. The very word sent shivers through their gizzards. The owls had long memories, and they each and every one recalled that in the old times the worst crimes and the most horrendous violence had happened under the name of "decency." It was power they all craved, not decency. Soren shut his eyes. His gizzard swirled with a nausea he had not experienced in years.

Otulissa lofted herself somewhat creakily into the air and settled on the wykensprat next to the warbler. She extended a wing as if to protect or perhaps support the small creature. "She actually called the bear stories fanciful and misleading?" the spotted owl asked, and Carrick nodded.

"I cannot imagine why she would do this. We all, all of us creatures, have our stories, legends. They not only inform us, they infuse us with spirit and strength. What possible reason would a creature have for trying to disgrace the bear legends?"

Soren began to speak slowly. "We build ourselves out of stories, and if you want to destroy a species, you would begin with the destruction of their legends. The bears were known for their stories. They never wrote them down — unfortunately — but despite being such solitary creatures, they told them to one another, perhaps through code, or way back before the Great Melting in that secret place where the Bear Council met. In every legend I do believe there is a truth struggling to get out. And sadly, there are legions of liars waiting to destroy that truth."

"When a creature loses its stories, it loses its courage," Otulissa murmured.

CHAPTER 11

Soldiers Together

Svenna sat at her desk in the harmonics lab, waiting for the sounds of the Mystress of the Chimes to leave. It seemed to be taking her a long time on this evening. But Svenna was patient.

Ever since she'd watched the little cub Juuls dissolve into a bloodstained mist, something had changed for her. She longed with almost a mother's desperation to find Juuls again and do what she could to help him.

Whenever the Mystress was absent from her den, Svenna would return to the hidden tunnel and search for Juuls in the darkness of the tunnel.

Finally she heard the sounds of the Mystress leaving. The tingle of the jewels that she wore to high meetings dissolved along with her footsteps, which were unusually light for a bear. Svenna opened the hidden panel and entered the tunnel.

Narrowing her eyes, she tried to scrape the shadows for the slightest hint of the tiny cub figure Juuls. Dare she call out? She slapped her paw to her mouth as one side of the tunnel's ice walls suddenly began to turn transparent. This had never happened before. Had she taken a different route in looking for Juuls?

Behind the wall, a bear was pacing the length of a large den with a sky port through which the stars radiated. This had to be the Stellata Chamber, where the most elite Timekeepers, the Gilraan, met, and this bear was none other than the Grand Patek. Svenna held her breath. What if he could see her? He was now directly in front of her on the other side of the wall, yet he didn't seem to register her presence.

Svenna exhaled and leaned forward for a closer look. The Grand Patek's robes were festooned with jewels. The glistening springs and spirals of myriad timepieces clinked as he swept from one end to the other of the Stellata Chamber, addressing the Gilraan. Among them were the Mystress of the Chimes, Master Udo, and the arrogant Torsenvryk Torsen, newly elevated to succeed the late Chronos.

"We are gathered here in the Stellata Chamber to welcome our new Chronos." The Grand Patek's high, shrill voice threatened to break into to a shriek. It reminded Svenna of the raspy edge of the katabatic winds in Ga'Hoole, winds so fierce they were rumored capable of stripping an owl in flight of its feathers. The Grand Patek paused momentarily to catch his breath.

"At the same time, we must remember the prophecy of the red comet. It was said that when it crosses the sky, only the faithless and the traitorous shall be plucked out. It was shocking to all of us that our late Chronos, Ivor Ahknah, was proven faithless.

"My Roguers reported that Ivor Ahknah was not the only bear purged by the comet. More than a dozen faithless bears of the Nunquivik were terminated in the glaring wake of the comet. You who still stand should be proud. You carry the badge of faith, of purity of heart and mind. You have faith, vrahkyn. And hence our sacred Ice Clock continues . . . Tick . . . Tock . . . Tick Tock . . ." He raised his forearm as he spoke and swung it as if it were a pendulum. The others began to chant and raised their forearms in a stiff salute and, mimicking their leader, began to swing them like a pendulum.

So he's blaming it on the comet, thought Svenna. *Make the comet the killer. Ridiculous!* This was exactly the kind of gobble-dygook that a false leader, a tyrant, would spew. Take a natural event and use it to justify an unnatural event like worshipping a stupid clock. Blame the comet for murder when Svenna knew in her deepest marrow that it was the Grand Patek who was responsible. Somehow Ivor Ahknah must have threatened the Grand Patek's power.

"But the comet," the Grand Patek continued, "only comes once every five years, and that is not often enough to eliminate the scores of other faithless who sought to destroy me and to destroy our beloved Ice Cap of the Ublunkyn, and have lapsed in their worship of our holy Ice Clock that shall deliver us from the floods of the Great Melting. Let me repeat. The faithful shall be saved. The toothwalkers shall cower before us. They shall turn docile as the white foxes to whom we toss our scraps. We shall eat the fat and blubber of the land.

"The faithless claim we 'steal their cubs.' We do not steal anything. We take in the name of the clock."

Svenna stood transfixed as she watched the Grand Patek rant. The members of the Gilraan stood in rapt attention, their eyes shining with admiration. And yet they were all blind. And their leader was mad. She had to get out. She must escape or she might grow as blind as the others.

"These faithless bears say terrible things about me that dishonor the clock. So I've sent Dark Fang to root out non-believers." The words *Dark Fang* caused a slight stir among the members of the Stellata Chamber. There was a new alertness. The Grand Patek paused for a few seconds, reveling in the impact of this announcement. "Yes, the Fang will find those who spread lies about the clock. He'll destroy all the faithless, all those *rebels*. He might have to go as far as the Northern Kingdoms. Perhaps all the way to the Great Ga'Hoole Tree. But by the clock, we shall rout out the faithless, be that creature bear or owl or wolf!"

"Brilliant!" cheered the new Chronos, Torsen, and clapped his paws. The other bears glanced at him nervously and then joined in the clapping and stomped their feet, cheering the Grand Patek on.

"Kill them!" they began to chant. "Kill the faithless!"

The Grand Patek raised his paw now for silence. "This time, Dark Fang won't let any of the rebels escape. We should've killed the Yinqui bear, Svern, instead of merely torturing him. We won't make that mistake again."

"Svern!" Svenna whispered. "They tortured Svern!" She felt herself wobble. She shut her eyes. In that moment she had one thought. She would escape and find her cubs, but not just escape — she would destroy this cursed place and its evil clock.

CHAPTER 12

Third's Dream

"They'll know him when they see him. They will know . . . Stormfast!" Third was muttering in his sleep.

"What's he saying?" Jytte asked as she and her brother watched Third stirring in his sleep, emerging from the depths of his walkabout dreams.

As Third neared the surface of the dream, the dense clouds of sleep began to thin. *I must tell them.* He began to speak with his eyes still closed, as if reciting from a well-known story.

"They will know. A wolf shall dwell with the seal, a toothwalker shall lie down with a fox, and cubs shall lead the way."

"Cubs?" Stellan repeated. He looked at his sister with alarm.

"You, the two of you," Third replied, now fully awake.

"Lead the way where?" Jytte asked. "We're looking, searching for the Den of Forever Frost. How can we lead any creature to any place?"

"Listen to me, cubs. In my dream, I saw that strange cub we met. She seemed to divide herself into two parts, or I should say two spirits, but I also saw an island. An island I had seen on Skagen's map. Remember Stormfast?" The cubs nodded. "Remember how the map was torn? A part was missing." Again the cubs nodded. "But in my dream, I saw the whole. I stood on that island, and across from it, I saw Bitter Sea and the Firth of Uthermere."

"Uthermere!" It was as if a spike of lightning had coursed through Jytte's body. "Uthermere was the firth of our father. It's nowhere near the Den of Forever Frost."

"Skagen said he wasn't entirely sure," Stellan said. "There's a chance that the Den of Forever Frost *is* near Uthermere. Is that where you think we should go, Third?"

Third looked down at his paws as if searching for an answer. "In my dream I met a bear, and she told me that we are in the wrong place."

"Did she tell you how to find our da?" Jytte asked eagerly.

"He's near Uthermere," Third said. "But I'm afraid . . . I think he might be lost."

"Lost?" Jytte repeated. "That makes no sense. If he's lost, then how can he be found in his old home in Uthermere?" Pain flashed across her face, as if she were imagining her father, the father she had never met, wounded and alone.

Third stepped closer. "I'm not sure, exactly. But I think I can find the way to Uthermere. You must trust my dreams and trust your stories."

Jytte and Stellan nodded. They would. They had been through so much together that their trust was as much a part of them as the blood that pumped through their hearts, the blood that streamed through their veins, and the stories their mum had told them. Those stories were not mere legends — they were waiting to be lived.

CHAPTER 13

We Mend the Broken

The cubs left the skunk bear's den and swam through a night and into a new day. They remembered studying the torn map and hearing Skagen tell them that Uthermere was west of the Everwinter Sea, south of Bitter Sea. A three days' journey.

The landscape became softer, less barren. A greening seemed to creep over the countryside, and even on the edge of the glaciers, tiny ice flowers often sprouted. The fish were plentiful, the seals less so. But there were succulent berries and roots and one particularly sweet flower they could not get enough of.

But Stellan knew that his sister hardly noticed any of this. Her thoughts had snagged on this notion that their father could be somehow lost. Lost and hurt and far away.

The day after Third's strange dream, they found themselves on the edge of a glacier. While they were feasting on the bright blue flowers that grew near the tip of the glacier, a tiny voice cried out.

"Oh no! Please. We need the honeyfrost for healing." The cubs turned to see where the voice came from. A spot of bright green sprang from the glacier, setting off a small explosion of crystals.

"Sylvia?" Stellan blurted out, crouching down to see if any creatures were tucked into a tiny crevice of ice barely wider than his claw.

"Sylvia? Who's Sylvia?" A green head popped up from the crevice.

"A frog just like you," Stellan said.

"Who are you talking to?" Jytte asked, coming over.

"A frog who looks just like Sylvia."

"Stellan, I don't think we should waste our time talking to frogs. We need to get on with it if we're going all the way to Uthermere."

"You obviously did not look at this frog Sylvia very closely," the frog said indignantly as he hopped closer to Stellan so they were muzzle to nose — although frogs did not exactly have a nose, Stellan realized.

"Stellan! Come on. We have to get moving. We don't have time to waste discussing if a frog is a he or she." His sister was radiating impatience. "But for your information, frog, Sylvia was a *Lithobates sylvaticus*, a wood frog. Now let's get out of here, Stellan."

"That might be, but she was not exactly like me, Miss Know-It-All. In our species, males are always smaller than females." The frog now drew himself up to his full height, which indeed was not very tall.

"How odd," Stellan said. He crouched down beside his sister for a better look. "That's not so with bears."

"STELLAN!!!" Jytte was ready to explode.

The frog ignored her. "I'm not a bear. You are so vain, so self-centered. You think all species must follow your rules."

"Well, no, not really —" Stellan said, but the frog cut him off.

"You haven't noticed that I am much more — how shall I put it — ornamented than your friend Sylvia. My skin is not simply green in color, but there are shades of azure and celadon." Stellan blinked. He had never heard of such colors. "Now please set down that honeyfrost blossom. I have a more worthy cause for it."

Third now stepped forward. "You said you need it for healing?"

"Yes, we are experts in mending the broken. Mending our kind as well as your kind."

"But we're bears," Third said.

"Yes, I realize that — the fur and the height were a give-away," the frog said somewhat sarcastically. "Indeed, I think I know the Sylvia to whom you were referring. Sylvia the diviner rhymer. The augur of the bog. The gazer in the maze. The seer who peers. So many names for her peculiar skills. That's the one?"

"Yes!" Stellan exclaimed. "She spoke in the strangest riddles."

"Too bad that her mate didn't listen to her. What a wreck he was."

"You . . . you . . . ," Stellan began to stammer. "She found his parts?"

"Indeed she did." The frog sighed. "The urge, you know. He didn't wait to thaw but broke out of his ice coffin too early. We helped her find his shattered limbs. But alas, I think it was too late. He's beyond the blessings of the honeyfrost. But there is another — one of your kind — that it might help."

"You mean a bear?" Jytte asked. A deep fear seized her. Could it be their father?

"Yes, a cub."

"But our kind don't shatter. We don't wait to thaw. Our blood runs warm all the time," Stellan said.

"Oh, there are many ways to shatter a creature. I believe this one was tortured."

Jytte gasped. Stellan knew what was going through his sister's mind. Jytte was picturing the Tick Tocks that Skagen had told them about who were brutalized by the Timekeepers at the Ice Clock.

"Could you come? Since this cub is your kind, it might make it easier," said the frog.

"But we're not healers like you," Stellan said.

"True, but you are large and strong, and there is something that you might be able to aid us in. Honeyfrost can only do so much."

Stellan caught Jytte's eye. If a cub was in trouble, they'd do what they could to help. "Show us what to do," Stellan said.

Night had fallen. The water was black, but the frog was like a glittering shooting star through the darkness of the night sea. However, with each stroke, Third began to feel a strange uneasiness.

Stellan sensed it immediately. Were they perhaps swimming into a trap? What if the frogs were working with Roguer bears? Myriad disastrous possibilities raced through Stellan's mind.

Just ahead, the frog stopped under the glacier wall that dipped beneath the water. "Come along! Come along!" the frog urged. "We have one of our kind who's taken a turn for the worse. Please!" The frog had lost all his cockiness. He was beseeching them to follow.

So they continued and dived beneath the glacier overhang, then surfaced on the other side. They were, in fact, in a dry glacial cave.

"What you call caves we call bores. Now follow me again and I'll take you to our ice clinic."

Third had started to shiver uncontrollably. "I . . . I'm afraid I can't continue."

Jytte and Stellan looked at their friend. They had never seen him like this before. They had faced Roguers, toothwalkers, all sorts of predators and dangers, but this was a different kind of fear.

"What's wrong, Third?" Jytte asked, extending her paw.

"I smell Taaka!"

CHAPTER 14

Twenty-Two Heartbeats Away

"Taaka!" Third repeated with a gasp.

"Your mother, Taaka?" Jytte asked. *Could Taaka have followed us all the way here? Why?*

"The frog said it's a cub. It can't be Taaka," Stellan said. Whoever it was, he sensed a fear in Third that was thickening like ice in the first of the seal moons.

"There is no full-grown bear in this bore," the frog assured them. "You have my word. My ice word that never thaws. Never changes. A cub has been brought in, a badly wounded cub. She is feverish. She will most likely die, but if we can get the honeyfrost to her, it's possible she might be saved. Follow me and you shall see."

Jytte and Stellan looked at Third, who appeared unable to move. "Third, it's a cub. You have nothing to fear. We'll be right beside you the whole time," Stellan promised.

"Come along, Third. We'll help you," Jytte said, putting a paw on his shoulder. Third looked into his friends' eyes, then nodded and allowed them to lead him forward.

The bore of the ice clinic was a peculiar place. There were ice shelves lined with shattered frogs whimpering and groaning in agony, all of whom had succumbed to the urge and broken out of their ice coffins before a true thaw.

They came to Sylvia around the next bend. They saw her body heaving. But there were no sobs coming from her, just a peculiar slime drooling from her lipless mouth and the sweet smell of the honeyfrost flowers. The limbless body of a frog was beside her. How could this be? Jytte wondered as she stared in horror.

"What is she doing?" Jytte asked frantically as she watched Sylvia applying the shimmering violet goo of the honeyfrost.

"She's trying to heal her mate, mend him with the honeyfrost. It's sticky, you see, and it can sometimes patch the limbs back together," said a nearby frog who was helping another patient.

At this moment Sylvia looked up at them. She wept huge sparkling tears that magnified her bulging eyes. "I have no riddles left. My dear mate no longer wants to live without his hind legs." Jytte felt a wrenching pain in her heart and clutched her own arm as if it might slip from her body.

Sylvia's mate let out a garbled croak. "He says to live without leaping is not a life for a frog." Sylvia began to shake. "But I would leap for him. I would . . . I would . . ."

"Come along, cubs. Leave her be at this moment." The frog turned. "My name, by the way, is Tyro."

It wasn't long before the bore widened. Ahead on a slab of ice they saw a mound of white fur. Its breathing was labored, and it too was moaning in pain. Third felt a shiver course through him.

"Second!" Third gasped. This cub was his next oldest sibling. Third was the tiniest of the lot, and his two older siblings, along with their mother, Taaka, seemed to derive a perverse pleasure from tormenting him. He had a scar on his foot where Second's tiny sharp teeth had bitten him. The fur had never grown in quite right, and the black skin was revealed.

Stellan felt a sickness roil through him as he looked at Third's sister, a bully who admired the savagery of her older brother.

"So that's what you call her — Second?" the frog asked.

"That is what Taaka called my sister, for she was second born."

"We believe in names and so have named her Froya."

"What happened to her?" Third asked, still staring at her numbly.

"She was found with another cub," Tyro began to explain. "A very badly wounded one whom she had trying to drag to safety from a gang of marauding bears. That cub died. It appears as if they tortured this one, Froya, trying to get information from her, then left her to die."

Third shuddered. As much as he loathed Second, he felt a twinge of revulsion at the word *torture*.

"Roguers, I suppose," Third whispered, feeling his terror grow at the idea of any bear being tortured.

"Oh, yes, definitely Roguers," Tyro replied.

Another anxious-looking frog had come up. "We were shocked," the frog began, and took a deep gulp of air. "Bears here in the Northern Kingdoms never attack their own, let alone cubs. Please let me pass through; I have some honeyfrost. It might help ease the pain in her shoulder."

His sister's arm dangled oddly at her side as her chest heaved with labored breathing. *She must be in terrific pain*, he thought. Unimaginable pain, much worse than when she had nipped his foot.

"Is it broken?" Stellan asked as a chill ran through him. How had these Roguers done that to the cub's arm?

"Not broken," the frog said. "But disjointed at the shoulder. We've tried shoving it back into the socket, but we're too small. We don't have the strength, but with your help we might be able to put the arm back into the shoulder joint. It's very painful, though the honeyfrost puts them into a deep sleep that erases pain."

Jytte and Stellan glanced at Third, who had retreated into a deep silence as he stared down at his erstwhile sister writhing in pain.

"Why do you call her Froya?" Third asked. He could not take his eyes from that oddly dangling arm. The cub was groaning in agony. Did she perhaps remember all the pain she had caused him? Did bullies ever think of that when they were suffering? "It's an unusual name," Third added, not shifting his gaze from his sister.

"Not in our world. Wood frogs have their stories and their legends just as the bears and the owls have theirs. This bear Froya was trying to rescue her yoonish."

"What's a yoonish?" Stellan asked.

"It's a frog word for leader, the tadpole that directs the others. Over the last several moons, there's been a stream of young cubs coming from the far, far north, the Nunquivik. But they are pursued by Roguer bears. Froya's yoonish was mortally wounded. That's who she tried to save. In the frog world, the yoonish is the frog who first figures out how to use a tail for navigation." The frog paused. His bulging eyes, cast down on the cub, were shining with admiration. "This valiant cub tried to save the life of her yoonish at the risk of her own."

Valiant? My sister valiant? Third thought.

"But why do you call her Froya?" Stellan asked. He sensed there was a story there.

"We call her that because she tried so hard to save the leader. She risked her own life. A most noble bear."

Noble bear! Third could hardly believe his ears.

"You see," Tyro continued, "in our frog legends, Froya was a hero frog, a beautiful frog goddess, known as the chooser of the slain — the nobly slain. She takes the most courageous warriors to the frozen ponds beyond the rainbow bridges in the Skaldsgard."

"Skaldsgard — that is your Ursulana, isn't it?" Stellan asked.

"Yes, our frog afterlife. The owls call it glaumora, the wolves of the Beyond call it the Cave of Souls, and we call it the Skaldsgard."

"Will she die?" Third finally spoke. It was harrowing to look at her, for the arm seemed completely separated from the shoulder and only connected by the fur. There was a deep dent, almost like a pocket, between the top of the arm and the shoulder that appeared askew.

Tyro took another gulp of air. "If her arm can be set to rights, she will no longer suffer, and then she might begin to mend and be able to eat. But it can't be set unless we give her the honey-frost, and then it will take more strength than all the frogs in this bore could ever muster."

Sylvia suddenly appeared.

"You're here?" Jytte asked.

"My mate is gone. He was beyond saving. I'm a widow now." She gave a little shake, as if she was trying to accustom herself to this new status. "I'm here to help."

She hopped onto Froya's chest and pressed her head against it. "Heartbeat weakening," she murmured.

"How many beats left?" Tyro asked

"Maybe twenty-five," Sylvia replied.

Stellan was astounded. "You can tell how many heartbeats a creature has before it dies?"

"You forget, my young friend," Sylvia said. "We are experts in dying. We die every winter. It is the waking up before the thaw that can be fatal for us. But this bear will die. Twenty-two more heartbeats and she is gone."

Stellan and Jytte looked to Third. It needed to be his decision, not theirs.

"Third?" Jytte asked softly. There was expectation in her voice. She simply could not believe that Third would allow this cub's agony to go on, but at the same time she felt it was wrong to push him.

Twenty-two heartbeats, thought Third. If she died, would he have to carry around this guilt for the rest of his life? It would be so easy to say, *No, let her go. She was horrible to me. She made my life miserable. I don't care if she dies.* But then that would be sinking to the level of that foul den of Taaka's. The evil of the den, like a rot, would have invaded Third.

"Give her the honeyfrost," Third ordered. "Stellan, you're the strongest, so when we're ready to shove her shoulder back into the socket, you brace her from behind her back, and Jytte and I will shove the shoulder."

"I shall begin the administration of the honeyfrost," Sylvia replied calmly. The bear's breath became shallow.

"How many more heartbeats, Sylvia?" Third asked.

"Eighteen. None to spare."

"Two to prepare ourselves," Jytte said. She was squinting at the strange disfigurement of the arm as if she were ice gazing.

Only in this case it wasn't ice she was gazing. It was bones. Jytte was trying to imagine how they fit together. How the arm lodged into the shoulder.

"On the count of five," Stellan said.

"One, two, three, four . . . five!"

CHAPTER 15

The Edge of Ursulana

Svenna hadn't been able to stop thinking about what she'd seen in the Stellata Chamber. The Grand Patek had actually been shouting out her mate's name. Svern! Bragging about torturing him. She pressed her paw to her heart and closed her eyes. Would they ever see each other again?

But there was nothing she could do to help Svern now. Her focus had to remain on escaping this wretched place and reuniting with her cubs. Though until she found a way out, she wanted to do whatever she could for the Tick Tocks. When she was sure no one was watching, she slipped back into the secret tunnel and wandered through the darkness until she saw the chillingly familiar bloodstained mist.

Them! It's them! A flood of gillygaskins roiled in the loom of the blood haze and the gillys seemed to be singing.

Drawn by their song, she began to make her way toward their voices.

At the edge of Ursulana,
Where the stars never shine,
Cling the gillygaskin cubs,
Far from that place sublime.
Oh, Ursus, let us in,
We're knocking at your door.
We must flee this cursed place,
Gather on that starry shore,
Though we're splintered,
And not whole.
We know that somewhere in this night,
Swirl the shards of our lost souls.

What gives wholeness to a life unlived?
A cub who's never played?
A creature snatched from mother's milk,
Her heartbeats muffled, then replaced
By ticks and tocks of that great wheel
That chews and rips and makes us bleed,
Yet never quite to die or live.
And so we're left behind,
To quivik we are doomed.
Suspended in our grief,

Ne'er to be alive or dead,
Between the fangs of time,
Nor glimpse Ursulana so divine.
Yet we long to see the stars bloom across the night,
To escape this bloody mist of quivik,
To take our final flight,
Through this never-ending night.

"Juuls? Juuls?" Svenna called out.

"Here," a tiny voice whispered. "Here with the rest."

There were so many of these gillygaskins, it was almost impossible to count them all. Perhaps one hundred or maybe five hundred. They loomed over this strange landscape. They did not appear to walk or crawl but float. Some lacked feet or paws. Sometimes they were headless, or a head might be drifting near the shoulders that it once set upon.

"But why, Juuls? Why can't you go to Ursulana?" Svenna asked. Juuls simply shrugged.

"I think . . . I think . . ." Another little gilly who was missing arms bobbed up and down through the hazy swirls. "We can't get to Ursulana because we aren't whole. We are so broken we don't even have shadows! If I could have my arms back and my legs, I could paddle, and then swim to Ursulana."

"No." Svenna shook her head. "You are not broken."

"But look at us!" a voice cried out. "I have no body. Just a head."

"You are whole inside. You were born whole, but you were all taken as Tick Tocks when you were too young to remember anything. Your mums, the milk, the winter den that first year. Did your mum ever tell you the story of the fidgety cub who could not be quiet during still hunting? Or the Ki-hi-ru stories? Did she tell you those stories about the shape-shifter foxes who can change themselves into other animals? Or dancing under the lights of the ahalikki? Did you ever do that?"

The armless gilly's head shook. Then the various other gillys shook their heads too, and murmured, "No . . . nooo."

"What's the ahalikki?"

How can I describe it? Svenna wondered. "It's sort of like a rainbow in the night."

"But what's a rainbow?" another asked, and before Svenna could begin to even try to explain, Juuls asked, "What are stories exactly?"

This shocked Svenna most of all. "What are stories? You don't know what a story is?"

"We know nothing except the escapement wheel."

Svenna looked out at the little ghost cubs. It seemed as if this place quivik was about as far from Ursulana as any bear could be. And why? They had hardly had a chance to be cubs.

"Can you show me the escapement wheel? If I am to understand you and understand this fiendish place, I must see the wheel on which you were imprisoned. I must understand your world if I am to help you get to Ursulana."

All she had to do was think of her own cubs, First and Second, that they would be here now if she had not come here herself to serve. These gillygaskins were her cubs now. These little ghosts who had been mutilated for this stupid clock were her mission now.

But Svenna herself was not a ghost. Not yet. She was alive, and her own cubs were alive somewhere, someplace. She knew that they had narrowly escaped from Roguers. As long as they lived, she was alive. She had the will to live and to do anything to escape. If she did, she knew where she would go. To the Northern Kingdoms to where the great bear Svree was said to have formed the first council of noble bears in the Den of Forever Frost before the Great Melting, before the time of the dragon walruses, before the monstrous tyranny of the Ice Clock of the Ublunkyn.

"Follow us," Juuls said. He and another cub began to lead Svenna through the vales of the murky blood fog. They came to a place of clear ice. Juuls pointed with his pawless arm. She realized that they were now on the back side of the clock, behind the clock face and peering into its innards. Her eyes focused on an immense wheel with sharp teeth spiking its circumference. There were notches between the teeth, each just wide enough to accommodate a very small cub, not even a yearling, just three or four months old. As the wheel turned, each cub hopped from one notch to the next.

"But what is the purpose?" Svenna asked, shaking her head in disgust.

"They experiment," Juuls replied. "Sometimes the wheel is fully loaded, each notch with a cub, sometimes not. It's all part of honoring the clock. It is an honor to sacrifice. That is what they tell us. It's proof of our faith, our vrahkyn."

Many of the cubs on the wheel were bleeding. Most of them were beyond being terrified. Their eyes seemed frozen and strangely clear — like ice. They were transfixed. They might as well have been dead.

"But why do they need to do this?"

"Balance. If the clock is balanced, they believe it gives warning of a great melting."

"Divine balance. That is what they call it," one gilly whispered.

"Divine! It's grotesque! It must be stopped," Svenna growled. "And it has nothing to do with faith."

Then the head of the headless cub floated close to Svenna and settled on her shoulder. The head spoke very quietly. "But we have been stopped. Stopped by death and stopped on our journey to Ursulana. We have not lived and we have not died exactly. We are caught on another wheel. The wheel of quivik, and we long to move on."

What the little gilly cub said struck Svenna deeply. The gilly was right. It was as if these poor creatures had been caught between the gears, the teeth of earth and the embrace of Ursulana. This was the meaning of quivik. But perhaps in some way she could help these cubs move on . . . move on to Ursulana.

"I must leave you now, but I shall be back. I promise."

Then Juuls gave a little chuff. "But what about stories? What are stories? You never told us."

"Stories are . . . Well, I'll have to tell you one when I come back. And I shall." Svenna paused. "But stories, yes, stories are important. You know, without stories a creature only lives one life, but with stories, a cub like you can live a thousand lives." She paused and took a deep breath. "'Once upon a time' are the most important words in any language."

"Not 'bless our clock divine'?" Juuls asked.

"Never!" Svenna replied fiercely.

And sometimes, Svenna thought, there was more truth in stories than in real life. These cubs had not had real lives. That was why their souls were restless. She had once said to Svern that stories could find dens in bears' souls. That was the first time Svern had hugged her. A warm feeling flooded through her.

I must tell them stories! Svenna vowed. *And when I send them on their way, then and only then shall I escape this place alive. I'll find my cubs and we shall go far, far away from the tyranny of this clock. This monster god!*

As Svenna was wending her way back to the Mystress of the Chimes's den, she heard another sound — peculiar and strange for this part of the world. She paused for a moment. It was like meltwater. *Impossible!* Nothing melted at the Ublunkyn. There was only *hyivqik* ice, the hardest kind that ran to great depths in this region, the most frozen part of the Nunquivik

Sea. To the south, one could often hear the growl of the sea beneath that ice. This sound, however, that Svenna was hearing was unnerving. It was as if something was tearing, ripping from the very core of the earth. *Perhaps*, Svenna thought, *Great Ursus herself was becoming angry at this infernal, savage Ice Clock!*

CHAPTER 16

The Last Heartbeat

"Now!" Third shouted as Stellan braced the dying Froya from behind. Jytte and Third both gave mighty grunts and shoved the arm into the socket. There was a popping noise.

"You did it!" Sylvia exclaimed. Tyro emitted a little yelp of joy as Sylvia pressed her ear slit to Froya's chest and listened intently. "The heartbeats are growing stronger. Strong as a frog in late-stage thaw . . . strong as a frog in midsummer . . . strong . . ." At that moment Froya's eyes opened.

She looked up at the three cub faces looming just above her own. Her eyes moved slowly from one to the other. Then she gasped as they settled on Third. "You!"

Third nodded slowly. "Yes, sister."

"You helped me?" Third nodded again. "But why? Why shouldn't you hate me?"

"I won't hate! Hate is for Taaka. Not me." Third took a deep breath, then whispered hoarsely, "I . . . I forgive you." The words that moments before had been like slivers of ice in his throat seemed to melt as he spoke them.

Froya shook her head slowly in dismay. "How could you?" Third was unsure himself. Could he say *I forgive you because I don't ever want to become what you were?*

But that would hardly be true forgiveness.

"You are a different cub now. The frogs told us how brave you were."

"What does that matter when I turned on you, my own brother?"

"You had a monster for a mother. How would you know better?" Third replied.

"But you knew better, Third."

Her body shuddered, and Stellan glimpsed the interior of her mind, which swirled with a barrage of horrific images of Taaka's rages. He saw gaping wounds that were bleeding. A cub knocked senseless by her huge paw and left outside the den. Froya began to sob.

"You see, first Taaka came after them, bullied Jytte and Stellan. She bullied them and I did nothing, for they were not of my blood. And then she came for you, Third, and still I did nothing. But I knew that she eventually would come for me. I heard her talking to the Roguers and I turned to my only brother and he did nothing. There was no one to defend me. But somehow I got away from them. You can't imagine how many cubs are being taken. I was one of the lucky ones. I joined a band of several cubs led by a strong young female — Lutta. We got far — all the way across the sea, hopping ice floe to ice floe, but they cornered us near the Firth of Grundensphyrr."

"How did you ever get here when you were wounded?" Stellan asked.

Tyro gave a loud croak. The cubs turned toward him. "When Froya tried to drag Lutta from the battle, she got her halfway into a cave before she died. It was a glacial cave. And glacial caves lead to glacial tunnels and crevasses."

"Is a crevasse underground like this bore?" Stellan asked, trying to understand the peculiar geography of this landscape.

"Not completely. Crevasses are cracks in the ice. One might be in a tunnel, but then suddenly the tunnel's ceiling opens up — just a slot — through which you can see the sky. There's a web of tunnels beneath these kingdoms that connect distant firths. If one can find one's way, it's quicker than crossing inlets, bays, or following coastal routes. The ice is often slick and the way can be very fast, faster than swimming or walking, but perhaps not flying. Yet who among us has wings?" Tyro looked about with his bulging eyes and emitted a series of gulps that the cubs realized was a frog's manner of laughing. "Not I!" He double-gulped at this. It was clear that Tyro considered himself quite the wit.

Jytte was more than impatient with this creature's so-called sense of humor. She needed to get him back on track. "We are searching for our father. We know that he came from the Firth of Uthermere. Do you know it?"

Stellan was actually happy that Jytte had not said the Den of Forever Frost. Since Grynda and the device in the cave, he was convinced that there must be spies in this country. The less said the better.

"Do we know Uthermere?" Tyro boomed. "Is a frog green or celadon or possibly azure? It's one of our favorite places to thaw."

"Could you direct us there by way of the tunnels and the crevasses?" Third asked eagerly.

"Of course!" Tyro began talking very fast. "You depart from here and head slightly east, but then you must turn west, bear north then angle south and . . ." Tyro was talking so fast the words were like a blur in the cub's ear.

"Wait! Wait! That's too fast," Stellan said. "Do you have a map?"

"Map?" Sylvia and Tyro both looked at each other in confusion.

"You know, it's . . . a . . . a . . ." Jytte began to speak but was not sure exactly how to describe a map to these creatures. Where would they have ever seen one?

Stellan interrupted his sister. "It's a drawing of how to get someplace, from one part of land to another. The sky with the stars is one kind of map. But if we're underground, we can't see the stars, or the land for that matter."

"Oh, indeed!" Tyro said. "Aha!" His eyes became quite

bulbous now as the meaning of the word *map* dawned on him. He glanced at Sylvia, whose eyes had grown equally plump as she sensed what a map was.

"What they need — would you not agree, Sylvia? — is a frost spider."

"Exactly."

"Frost spider? Third repeated. "How can a spider help us?"

Sylvia appeared to shrug. "It's not all about size, you know. Frost spiders know this underground world better than any creature, and they will know how to guide you."

But Third, of course, had merely spoken what Stellan and Jytte were thinking. How could a creature as tiny as a spider guide them? Stellan was fearful that they might accidentally step on such a minuscule guide and squash it.

"They know the way. They are your living map as good as the stars. They can guide you," Tyro said.

Jytte tried to quell her growing excitement. If these strange spiders could actually guide them to her father, and if they could do it by traveling underground and dodge Roguer bears . . . Dare she hope? "But will they agree to guide us?" Jytte asked.

"Oh yes, they are proud of their skills. Proud of their silk. You see, in their webs they spin designs, rather like these drawings you spoke of — the maps of the stars and the land. They will spin you the silk and weave you a picture. They are industrious little creatures. Just start following this branch of the tunnel and within a short time you will find one who will be happy to guide you."

Jytte and Stellan both felt a rush of anticipation. If the spiders could actually spin them a map, there might be a way for them to get to Uthermere without being intercepted by any Roguer bears.

"There will be more than one, really, Tyro," Sylvia corrected him.

"Oh yes. True. The first spider spins a web that you can follow for a distance. Then when you come to the end of that course, there will be another spider who can take up the task. They're very trustworthy and will warn you of dangers. Remember, spiders have eight eyes. All-seeing!"

"What dangers?" Stellan asked, trying to imagine what kinds of dangers could be lurking in this tunnel.

"Well," Sylvia said slowly, "there is another creature in the tunnels that is quite vicious." Sylvia seemed to be hesitating.

"Come on," Jytte urged. "Out with it. Tell us. We've encountered vicious creatures before."

"Frost vipers." She clamped her bulgy eyes closed as she said the words. It was almost as if it pained her to name them. "They are deadly to milk creatures but not to us."

"And these frost spiders can warn us of the vipers?" Third asked.

"Yes. The spiders have exceptional hearing. They can detect a slither. That is what they call a mass of the frost vipers — a slither. There can be as many as one thousand vipers in a single slither."

"How could we ever escape that?" Stellan gasped, incredulous.

"It's not the slither that is the problem. But if a single viper breaks away, that snake becomes extremely vicious. Its venom becomes even more toxic. An animal bitten by that one viper dies within seconds."

"Are you sure you want to go?" Sylvia asked.

"Yes," the three cubs replied at once.

"I want to go too," Froya said softly. Jytte looked at the cub, startled. Her arm restored to its proper position looked normal, but was she strong enough to go? Would she slow them down? They couldn't afford to waste any more time.

"Why do you want to go?" Jytte asked. "He's not your father."

"I want to be among good bears. You are good bears. Your father must be a good bear, as was your mum, Svenna." There was a quiet dignity to her words. An unshakable yet simple honesty.

Third had many of the same questions as Jytte. Was it really fair of him to endanger their mission? But then he thought about what Sylvia had told them, how Froya put her own life at risk to protect the other cubs. For his forgiveness to be genuine, he needed to give her a second chance.

"Of course, Froya, you may come. But do you feel strong enough?" Third asked.

"I am strong enough."

Jytte and Stellan exchanged nervous glances.

"I'm not sure if this is the best idea," Stellan said. "You were badly injured, Froya. How do you know if you'll be able to keep up with us?"

Froya tried to stand straight. Her arm still ached, but she willed herself not to hold it as if she were protecting that shoulder again. She must appear strong and fit and ready to be of help.

"I . . . I don't want to be left behind. You have one another. But . . . but . . . who do I have?" The guard hairs on her muzzle seemed to quiver.

"Me," Third said firmly. "You have me." He then turned to Stellan and Jytte. "If you insist on leaving Froya, I'll stay. She is my sister. My blood."

Jytte's eyes opened wide. "Really, Third?"

"Really, Jytte," Third replied.

"Then we all go," said Stellan said firmly, without a second's hesitation.

"Thank you." Froya spoke softly.

The frogs had not said a word during this exchange. In fact, they seemed to be holding their breath. A large bubble of air issued from Tyro's mouth.

"Well now, cubs. Follow me and I shall introduce you to your first guide. Her home web is just around the next bend."

CHAPTER 17

The Way of the Silk

Stellan was in the lead as the cubs made their way through a tunnel sheathed in frost. Tyro had told them that they would meet their initial frost spider guide at the first bend. Jytte pushed her doubts about Froya from her mind. She would let nothing distract her from their mission. The air was dry and tingly on the cubs' noses. Jytte sniffed. The air did not smell of the sea, or salt. It smelled like no place — no place they had ever been, and about as far from a bear place as one could imagine.

The cubs sensed a stillness that they were not accustomed to. But the tunnel did feel safe, insulated against the dangers of the world above.

They had not traveled far when they spied a sparkling web ahead. Its silk threads shimmered in the darkness. Stellan opened his eyes wide. It was as if a constellation had fallen from the sky into this dark tunnel. And gleaming like a gem in the very middle of the web was a large spider.

"Pekka is my name," she announced before they could even ask who she was. Her eight black eyes sparkled as she tipped the front part of her body. This would have been a gesture similar to nodding if indeed her head had not been fused to the rest of her body. As she appeared neckless, it was difficult to see where in fact her head ended and the rest of her body began. "The wood frogs refer to us as frost spiders," she said. "However, as you can see from my exterior, we are in fact quite colorful, and many refer to us as jewel spiders. We are part of the orb weavers' branch of the spider family and are known for our intricate web designs. But I shall try to keep things simple for you so you can follow the threads easily. This first web shall take you quite a way, at least to King's Crossing."

"Why do they call it that? Do you spiders have a spider king?" Jytte asked. She was uncertain where to look, as trying to focus on all eight eyes was a bit disorienting.

"Oh, no, not a spider king at all. It's named for the owl H'rath, the old king of the Northern Kingdoms, the N'yrthghar, as it was called back then. At King's Crossing you shall be met by another spider who will spin a web directing you to the next waystation, Svenka's Landing."

"Svenka!" Stellan exclaimed. "Our mum told us that we were descendants of a hero bear named Svenka."

"Indeed, she was a hero. She helped rescued H'rath's queen,

Siv. Owls and bears often worked together in the old days. This journey that you are about to embark upon is, in a sense, a history of those old legends. Svenka's Landing is, of course, on the land above this tunnel."

"This spider knows so much," Froya whispered to her brother, clearly impressed.

"How will the next spider know we are coming?" Jytte asked.

"Ah! Excellent question, young'un. Freeriders, or sometimes called *sellsilk*. I shall send a message ahead."

"How?" Jytte asked.

"I'll twang it. It's a method of communication we use. We pluck very lightly on a taut thread in our webs, which creates vibrations. It's a code of sorts. I should warn you: These sellsilks will try to sell you some of their silk. They spin a very high grade. It has a variety of uses, including binding wounds, for it can stop bleeding."

All while Pekka talked she spun the web map. The silk was luminous, and in the shadowy tunnel the route glowed with a bright radiance that gave the cubs hope. But the bluish ice in the glacial tunnel was very different from any they had known. Jytte studied it hard. She could normally perceive any ice's particular traits. She knew if it was brittle, or fast ice, or hyivqik. She knew if it harbored invisible air bubbles that made the ice very hazardous. She understood how the crystals fit together to form each kind of ice. But this ice, she didn't understand. "I have never seen ice like this," she said, more intrigued than worried.

"Glacier ice is just packed snow," Pekka explained. "It's not true ice. But it is my web that you need to observe, not the ice. Study it hard and keep the image in your mind's eye, cubs. Your memory of my web will guide you. Now, your last stop before ascending will be Pleek's Plonk. That is a crevasse, and you must exit the underground from there. It's right at the center of the Uthermere crevasse and one of the most wooded areas in Uthermere on Stormfast Island."

Uthermere — the very name thrilled Stellan and Jytte.

"Now, this is where your first big turn is," the spider said, pointing with one of her rear legs as she suspended herself upside down. "You turn there, and then up there is where you'll meet your next guide."

She indicated this spot with the opposite leg. She was quite agile.

"She can really move, can't she?" Jytte marveled quietly.

"Eight legs do help!" Third whispered.

The cubs then fell silent as their eyes moved over the burnished silken threads, studying the path.

As they bid Pekka good-bye, they each tried their best to keep the image of the web in their mind's eye. They would begin their journey by turning east in the tunnel for a short distance, then forking to the west.

They proceeded silently though the tunnel unfurling before them. Sometimes the passage grew quite narrow and other times it was wide enough to walk side by side. There were sudden dips where the cubs were forced to grip with their claws to avoid skidding. And oftentimes the path would bend sharply, and they would encounter a blind turn or a fork. Jytte was now leading, concentrating deeply to keep the silken map firmly in her head.

Third was pleased that Froya could be keep up, and that the cubs had put aside — or so it seemed — their hesitations about his sister joining them. But how long could they avoid sharing their true destination with Froya? How much did she know about the Ice Clock? She knew about Roguers, but did she know what they did to cubs, the ones called Tick Tocks, at the Ice Clock?

Froya herself just seemed happy to be with them. Third looked back at her. It was as if Froya's mind shimmered with the pulsing lights of the ahalikki. *The Belong*, thought Stellan. *She feels The Belong.* That was what Third had said when he joined Stellan and Jytte after escaping from Taaka. *Nobody has ever cared for me at all until you two came along. I feel The Belong.*

There was a difference between being above the glacier and being beneath it. It was a windless world, a world of ice and shadows. A world unsuspecting of day or night, heedless of seasons. It was a deep, narrow world with no horizons. That, perhaps, was the hardest for the cubs. Earth without horizons was no world at all.

But the cubs trudged on. Jytte was still in the lead. She called back, "I think we might be approaching King's Crossing. Remember in the web map there was a place where the path narrowed and made a sharp turn?"

"Yes," Third replied, emitting a sigh of relief.

"Oh, we're here!" Jytte cried out. "King's Crossing."

An iridescent spider with sparkling flecks of silver swung through the air like a tiny errant star from the world above.

"Welcome. I already have the web spun for your perusal. But in addition, I have some artwork if you would have time and wit to appreciate it." The spider nodded toward another web with a very intricate design.

"What do you mean wit?" Jytte said, bristling. "You think we're stupid?" Stellan placed his paw on his sister's shoulder. He knew all too well how easily Jytte's temper could be roused.

"Steady, Jytte."

"I am steady. This spider just insulted us."

The spider gave a slight shiver. The silvery flecks of his carapace blurred momentarily. "I just meant that there is more to life than getting from here to there. You must leave time for art."

"Over there, sir?" Stellan asked, pointing to a web, not sure if that was the art web or the one below it.

"Sir! Now, indeed, you are ignorant! I am a female." Her eight shiny black eyes flashed. "You can't see that egg sac woven into my art web? I always weave a masterful design to conceal the egg sac of my babies. I have even been called upon to weave concealment designs for other spiders' egg sacs."

Third stepped forward. "Your cubs are in there?"

"My unborn young are in there, and they are not called 'cubs.' Bears, yes, are the largest predators on earth, but it's not all about you! When my 'cubs,' as you call them, hatch, they will become known as spiderlings."

Stellan felt that things were spiraling out of control. Somehow within a very short time the cubs and the frost spider had managed to insult one another. He peered at the spider suspended on a glistening violet thread from the map web she had just completed for the cubs.

"Ma'am, forgive our rough ways. My name is Stellan. This is my sister, Jytte, and this is Third and Froya. What, may I ask, is your name?"

"Akka. I am named for a sacred tree."

"Are there trees down here?" Third asked curiously.

"Of course not."

"But your mother named you for a tree?"

Sometimes Stellan wished that Third would not get caught up with such small details. He could feel Jytte growing impatient.

"My mother did not name me," Akka said. "That would be an impossible task."

"Why?" Third asked.

"If you hatched over five hundred cubs, would you be able to think up five hundred names? Of course not!"

Jytte's interest was instantly snagged. "Are you telling me five hundred spiderlings are in that sac?"

"More or less. That is why they must name themselves."

"We have something in common, Akka," Stellan said. "My sister and I named ourselves as well."

"And for what are you named?"

"The stars," Jytte said proudly.

"The stars, interesting. And are there stars on land?"

"Of course not," Jytte said. "They're in the sky."

"My point precisely. Can you touch them? Hold them in your hands? Certainty not! No more than I can climb from these tunnels and spin a web in an Akka tree, but I can imagine. Now, I should explain this web for you so you can get on from here to your next waystation in Uthermere."

"No," Stellan said, and held up his paw. "Let's first see your art, the web with the concealed egg sac. I can now see from here it is very beautiful."

All eight of Akka's eyes brightened.

"I would be most happy to show you." She swung up to the top of the webs that concealed the egg sac. "Here you see, or barely see, my egg sac." She paused. "That, my friends, is the future!" There was a note of triumph in her voice. Then she cast another silk thread, a turquoise one, with which she began to rappel down the steep face of the web, and moved across to the other side of the web. "I am now in the region of the eastern latticework made with a high-quality but less flexible silk, and the images represented here are . . . Well, you tell me."

The cubs stepped up closer and began to examine the web.

"See anything familiar?" Akka asked.

"That one looks like an owl." Third pointed with his claw. "The other one looks sort of owlish but wrong somehow."

Akka lowered her voice to an almost conspiratorial level. "Indeed, cub, these owls are dreadfully wrong."

"Why?" Froya asked, her voice trembling.

Stellan frowned. "Are they the same, hagsfiends and haggish owls?"

"Not exactly. Let me pose this question: Are toothwalkers and dragon walruses the same?"

Stellan winced, reliving the pain in his haunch where months before the attacking toothwalker had snagged him, tearing deep into a tendon.

"No," Akka continued. "Toothwalkers of today are not exactly the same as dragon walruses of the Long Ago, of legend." She paused. "But they were not simply legend. They were a spawn of *nachtmagen*, a magic that is like a disease of those who crave power. Hagsfiends as well were relic creatures that had acquired destructive powers. And they had a peculiar talent. In the old days, they spun webs . . . but with their eyes. It was not a web of silk but of light. It was called a *fyngrot* and it paralyzed its victim. Perfect for trapping owls. Their wings would lock and they would plummet to the ground in flight. Or in the language of owls, they would go yeep. But eventually the hagsfiends died out, became extinct, and yet . . ."

"And yet what?" Third asked.

"They left their traces behind, just as the dragon walruses left their traces. The toothwalkers are not as monstrous as their predecessors and not as big as you bears, but you must admit they're a danger to you."

"Definitely," Stellan replied. "But my question is, what are the traces left by the hagsfiends?"

"The frost vipers, of course," Jytte replied.

"But a snake is so different from a bird," Stellan said.

"Ah yes," Akka sighed. "But listen to me, cubs. In the Long Ago, before the forms and the shapes of creatures had been set, there might have been some connection. It was a question that the screech owl Ezylryb, the sage of the Great Ga'Hoole Tree, had begun to study shortly before his death." Akka paused. "Now you know, of course, that as a slither, the frost vipers are not dangerous. It is only if one breaks from the slither. Then it will attack. But don't worry."

"Don't worry!" Jytte blurted.

"This time of year, they are mostly intent on getting to their feeding grounds to the south. They have one single collective mind that tells them what to do. The risk to them is greater than for you. You see, if they break from the group and attack some creature, they die immediately after they strike."

"I don't find that especially comforting, Akka," Jytte replied.

Akka appeared to shrug, as much as a spider can shrug. "Now, my next piece is an homage." She was making her way to a third web. "Homage to the Great Marven."

"Marven!" Stellan exclaimed. "So he *was* real."

"How could you ever doubt it?"

"We didn't." Third stepped forward. "But there are others who did."

"Many creatures prefer ignorance to knowledge. It is very easy to vanquish with ignorance. That's why I am an artist. I spin the tales of history. And let me tell you that Marven is part of your history. The dragon walruses he vanquished were not mere legend. Nor was Marven. As you continue to Uthermere, you will see more of my webs along the way." She waved several of her legs about. "I consider this glacier tunnel my gallery!"

Jytte leaned forward into the darkness ahead. She couldn't care less about Akka's gallery. All that mattered was getting to Uthermere and finding her father. "What about the map that will show us the way to Uthermere? That is why we are here."

"Oh yes, of course, silly me. Nearly forgot the reason for your visit. Do take a look at the web I have woven to show you your course." As they watched, she spun out a silken thread and swung across to another in a high corner, pointing out various features in the map along the way. The cubs tipped their heads back and studied the web.

"There's a major branching point fairly soon after you leave here," Akka continued. "Take this one." She climbed over toward the point in the web where two threads split and plucked one. "That's the branch to take." She flashed all eight of her eyes and began waving at least six of her eight legs about.

"Yes," Stellan replied, staring at the dazzling display. "We won't miss it."

CHAPTER 18

The Sellsilk

The cubs said good-bye to Akka. Jytte insisted on leading. She had been very impatient with Akka and her art, but Akka's map was by far the best. It confirmed that they really could get to the firth where their father had come from.

The cubs felt a new certainty in their progress, and yet despite the colorful webs there was a monotony to the tunnel.

"I love Akka's art," Stellan said suddenly. "But you know what I would love even more?"

"What?" Third asked.

"To see night . . ." Stellan paused. "Or day. To know when it is night or day. To see real light and not just the shimmering colors of these spiders' webs."

"To see an ahalikki?" Jytte said. "Now that is art! And no creature made it!"

Froya tugged lightly on Third's tail.

"What is it, Froya?"

"I'm hungry," she whispered.

"Why are you whispering?"

"I don't want them to know."

"What are you talking about?"

"They'll think I'm weak. I'm trying to be strong. I don't want them to leave me."

"They won't. They know that you're part of me. We're together. But we've got to keep you fed!" Third said this with sudden urgency. He turned and called to Jytte and Stellan, who were several paces ahead. "Hey, we're hungry! You realize we've only had two voles in the last —"

"You see, that's the problem." Jytte huffed. "We don't know day from night. We can't keep track of time."

"My stomach can," Froya muttered.

"How far until our next guide?" Stellan asked.

"Not far," Jytte said. "Oh, cubs!" she shouted. "Good news." They heard a resounding smack. "Vole in a hole!" she cried out gleefully.

Third and Froya scrambled to catch up. The cubs began swatting the tiny rodents with their paws and knocking them senseless. Even though Froya could only use one of her arms, she was quick.

"Good work, Froya!" Stellan said.

"Really?" It nearly broke Stellan's heart to see how pleased she was. She was really just a cub like them. He must forget that she had once bullied her younger brother. He decided right then to tell Froya about their mission.

"Froya," Stellan began.

"You're not going to leave me, are you?" She had never heard Stellan sound so serious, almost severe.

"No, no, of course not." Stellan took a deep breath. "Froya, you are part of a mission."

"You mean to find your father, Svern?"

"Well, it's really larger than that." He glanced at Jytte. She nodded. He felt better. *Go ahead*, she seemed to say.

"You know about the Roguers, of course."

"Yes," Froya answered in barely a whisper. "They capture young cubs and take them away to serve at the . . ." Her voice dropped. "At the Ice Clock." She could barely say the words. "They do bad things to cubs there."

"Yes," Stellan replied. "And that is our mission. To stop the clock and destroy the Grand Patek's power."

"How can you stop it?"

"Our father will help us. He's a famous rebel who once came close to destroying the clock."

All the cubs kept their eyes on Froya. She did not speak for a while but looked at her paws, studying them intently.

"I have heard of this bear, Svern," Froya said. "He was a leader of the rebellion. But then he disappeared. Some say the Roguers killed him. But others say he escaped the black ice cells, the orts, they call them."

Stellan saw Jytte begin to tremble. "Don't worry, Jytte. He probably escaped, as Froya said."

"But how will we ever know?"

"All the more reason for pushing on and getting to Uthermere."

"But when will this tunnel ever end? There's no way to tell if we're getting close. Down here, the ice never changes. There aren't any seasons."

"Ahem!" A sound like tiniest sneeze in the universe came right out of the ice floor of the tunnel. "Now that's where you're wrong!"

The cubs all swiveled their heads. "Who said that?" Jytte called.

"Me!" The voice was very close to where she sat. She looked down at the ice. There was a crack between her knees. "And please don't move, else you'll squash me." All four cubs looked down now. There was something trying to get out of the crack. First one leg came, then two, then another and another. And . . .

"I'm here!" the voice declared. "Who said that bit about no seasons here?"

"Me," Jytte said.

"You're wrong. We are just now entering the season of the weeping ice."

"Are you sure?" Jytte asked. "Are we getting toward the end? Are we closer to Uthermere? What does it mean?"

"It's weeping ice! That's what it means. Please note how slick the ice has become. The walls of the tunnel are weeping."

The cubs looked at the walls. They did seem to shimmer. Froya swiped her paw across the surface.

"Not exactly wet. But clammy," she reported.

"Yes, clammy. It's going to be slippery going for a while. But I can provide you with a triple-ply rope made of highest-quality silk from my port spinnerets, one and two, combined with my grade-A multi-use silk from my celebrated starboard third spinneret. This line is unequaled in a variety of situations, as it provides a shock-absorbent core and can be combined with my number one and two port spinnerets' silk for a braided sheath. And let's not even talk about the tensile strength. Woo-hoo!" the spider exclaimed, and appeared to roll all eight of his eyes, which from the cubs' perspective was incredibly dizzying.

It dawned on Stellan that this spider must be a sellsilk.

"But why would we need this, and how could it ever support a bear?" Jytte asked.

The spider sighed, then began to speak with an exaggerated patience. "I know, I know, 'largest predators on earth.' But believe me, when you get to Pleek's Plonk, that's how you'll ascend on my very best silk to Uthermere, my dear."

"What do you mean?" Froya asked. Her voice was slightly quavery.

"Go up. Climb. Although you have only four appendages while I have eight."

"I think that's why I'm sort of . . . well, nervous," Froya said.

Third patted her good shoulder. "You can do it!"

Froya blinked rapidly. "Of course. Of course." She knew she shouldn't have mentioned that she was nervous. Would they leave her behind?

"Why do they call it Pleek's Plonk?"

"'Plonk' is the operative word here. The important one. You see, many, while climbing out, have gone plonk. Plonk as in splat. Fall down flat. And in this season of the weeping ice, 'tis best to have a good, strong, tested triple-ply rope spun by yours truly here, Knute of the Ironsilk clan of frost spiders. So I would advise that you purchase some silk from me."

"We have nothing to buy with," Third said.

"But you do," Knute said. "Your claws."

"Our claws?" Jytte asked nervously, glancing down at her own curved black claws.

"You see that crack next to the one I just came out of?"

Jytte squinted. "There's a crack there?"

"That's the problem. It's so tiny as to be almost invisible. But there is one. Believe me."

"I guess eight eyes are better than two," Third said.

And eight appendages better than four, Froya thought.

"It's not really my eyes that see it. It's the hairs on my legs. Or fur, you might call it." The spider lifted two of its legs. There were tiny bristles.

"Seeing fur!" Stellan exclaimed. It was the most peculiar notion in the world that a creature could see with its fur, or bristles, or pelt, for that matter.

"It's feeling, not seeing. I can feel vibrations, and I know there are ice worms there. If you can pry that crack open with one of your claws, that would mean a feast for me and silk for you."

"But how will we see it?" Stellan asked.

"Easy! I'll spin out one of my most luminous threads — Breaking Dawn Scarlet, I call it. I'll lay it down right on the crack, and you can follow it. You just drag your claw along that thread and that will do it. I have a web ready to receive them." He nodded toward a pale latticework that was suspended near the floor of the tunnel.

The cubs exchanged glances. Third nodded.

"Easy enough," Third said. "I'll do it. I have the smallest claws. Mine will probably work best."

In no time Knute had laid down a track of Breaking Dawn Scarlet silk.

"All right." Third inhaled deeply and crouched down. He began dragging his pinkie claw along the line. Almost instantly, half a dozen little ice worms wriggled out. Knute was all action. He swung in on a thread of gray silk from his web and seized four ice worms, two with his front legs, then swiveled and grabbed two more with his rear legs. Then he was back in the web. He began spinning a green thread. "Binding silk specially concocted for ice worms." The worms were wiggling a bit. "Settle down, fellows. It'll be over soon."

The cubs stood by in amazement. Within a very short time, Knute had a dozen ice worms bound up in his web.

"That ought to do it. Got my summer food supply. And a deal's a deal. So I'll accompany you to Pleek's Plonk and spin you the strongest ascent line ever! There shall be no plonking. My word of honor." The tiny frost spider seemed to take a bow from his web.

Stellan felt reassured that Knute had enough food to guide them on for the rest of the route. "And how far is it to Pleek's Plonk?" he asked.

"Not far. Not far at all, and I shall go with you. I know the ice. I know how it changes along this route. I can even tell time by the ice, for I know the sound of the ice when it's morning above, and then just after the noon when the sun starts to slip away, and finally when the moon rises."

"And I thought I knew ice," Jytte said. "They call me an ice gazer, but I guess I can understand it only when I am above-ground, not below."

"You would learn if this were your world. And soon we'll enter a crevasse."

"A crevasse?" Stellan exclaimed. "That's when we'll see the sky."

"Exactly."

The four cubs had a single thought: *How wonderful to see the sky!*

CHAPTER 19

Pleek's Plonk

As the cubs rounded a bend, they gradually became aware that there was a different quality to the darkness. Each one seemed to sense it but dared not say a word until finally Jytte stopped. She realized that the ice *did* feel different and it had to be light that had changed the ice, and yet it still seemed dark in the tunnel.

"Let me go ahead of you, Stellan." She had not gone more than a few steps when she cried out, "Sky! I see sky."

"Yes," Knute said calmly as he swung on an orange thread above them. "We are entering the crevasse."

The crevasse was narrow, but when the cubs looked up, they saw a sliver of blue over their heads. Soon the crack opened wider and the sliver of blue became a ribbon unfurling above them.

"A cloud!" Jytte cried. A gossamer white cloud stretched out against the blue. "Look! It's racing across the sky. There must be a breeze. A breeeeeze!" She stretched out the word as if she were tasting it, and it was the most delicious thing in the world after this endless journey beneath the ground where a wind never blew.

"A bird! Not an owl. Maybe an eagle?" Stellan said as a bird slipped from the cloud and angled its wings. It was as if the cubs were reclaiming, piece by piece, a world they knew.

They kept walking. Their progress was slow, as the cubs rejoiced with every treasure the sky revealed after their days of endless bareness in the depths of the glacier tunnel.

They whispered with delight as the day above faded into the dusky colors of twilight and then caught their breath when they spied the first star.

"We're here," Knute said quietly.

"Pleek's Plonk?" Froya asked.

"Yes, and it's time for me to get to work spinning a silk ladder for you."

The cubs looked up. It was hard for them to imagine Knute spinning a rope that would reach to the top.

"Can you really do that, Knute?" Stellan asked doubtfully. What if this silk began to shred and they fell? It would be a long fall. They might not get hurt, but how would they ever get out? The thought of staying beneath the ground forever was not a pleasant one.

"Yes, but let me explain. As you can see, there are some pawholds in this ice wall left from other creatures making their ascent. You must use both the ladder and the pawholds. But at this time, the time of the weeping ice, the pawholds are not reliable. Your paws and feet can slip. So the rule here is one paw for the holds and one paw for the ladder. Do you understand?"

The four bears nodded.

"I should have the ladder completed by the time the Aranea rises in the sky."

"Who?" Froya asked.

"Aranea, the Great Spider constellation."

The ladder, spun in shades of green and blue and soft pink, was a glorious creation. As Knute wove the last rung, he called down.

"Aranea rises!"

The cubs crowded together at the base of the silk ladder and gazed up into the night.

"Beautiful," Froya whispered. There was one bright blue star, Aranea, in the center, but a mass of hundreds of stars spread out from it, forming a web across the night sky. The cubs couldn't even see the far edges of the Aranea constellation.

"Now, I suggest you start up one at a time. The ladder is strong, but all of you at once might be too much."

"You're the smallest, Third," Stellan said. "Why don't you go up first?"

"Are you sure, Stellan? Maybe since you're the biggest we should test it with you."

"I might strain the ladder too much. Better to get the lightweights up first — you and Froya. Then Jytte and I will follow."

"I suppose," Third said reluctantly.

The cub stretched up and reach for the pawhold just above his head and then placed one foot in the foothold. With his free paw and free foot he reached for a rung of the ladder and tugged it a bit as a test. Then he put his foot on a lower rung.

"Seems to be holding," Third said, though there was a tentative note in his voice. "Of course, I'm the smallest. So maybe it's not a real test."

"Come along, come along," Knute said. "We don't have all night."

Stellan detected a new urgency in the spider's tone. Was Knute doubting his creation?

Third made it to the top. He shut his eyes for a brief moment and emitted a sigh of relief.

"Good, good job. Quick now, Froya," Knute snapped.

Stellan felt a trickle of anxiety. *This spider is fearful of something.*

Stellan's riddling powers began to stir, picking up the scents of Knute's alarm. The spider was worried about the ladder, but something else too. Terror was flooding through the spider's mind.

Stellan looked over his shoulder as he stood at the bottom

of the ladder. A dark river seemed to be oozing toward them, and then he blinked in horror as he saw the molten red eyes of what could only be frost vipers. "A slither!" he shrieked. "Go! Go, Jytte."

"But Froya hasn't reached the top," Jytte shouted.

"Never mind. Go! Go!" Knute and Third were both yelling. Then Knute swung down on a thread, landing on the wall between Froya and Jytte, who had just started climbing. "Quickly, quickly. Don't panic. We're all right unless one breaks away. Steady there, Jytte. Froya, you keep going. Never look back."

The moment he uttered those words, there came another sound. A hissing. One viper had broken free of the slither and was racing across the weeping ice toward them. Jytte saw it too. She began to back down the ladder. A flood of terror swept through her, and she felt as if she were being engulfed by the red glow of their eyes.

"No!" Stellan and Knute both cried. But Stellan couldn't step on the ladder yet, as it would certainly be too much weight, and Jytte now seemed frozen, unable to move.

"You have to go, Jytte." Knute voice was strained. "I can't cast until you've cleared the way for Stellan."

Cast? Stellan thought. *Why is he casting? The ladder is made.*

Jytte finally moved again and Stellan began to climb up the ice wall. The viper started to coil. Its head was just beneath Stellan, its forked tongue lashing out. At that moment, Knute unleashed a massive amount of silk, which landed on the viper's head, then wrapped around its body. Stellan's breath locked in his throat as he watched a knot in the silk begin to tighten. The viper was retching, its red eyes bulging and growing dimmer as if a fog had rolled across them.

But there was another sound too — weak gasping. Stellan sensed it before he saw what was happening. It was the sound of a spider dying. Knute was dangling feebly from one of the silken threads.

"Knute?" There was no answer. "Knute, are you . . . are you . . ."

The spider stirred just a bit. "I gave it my all, Stellan. All of my silk."

"Knute, you can't die." Stellan felt desperation invade him. *No, you can't! A creature so far from our own kind shouldn't die for us!* But the spider already had, and dropped from the thread to the bottom of the crevasse, where the frost viper lay dead, wrapped in the snare of silk that Knute had spun.

Guilt and sorrow weighed heavy in his heart as Stellan began to climb. His paw nearly slipped, as the ice wall was weeping steadily, and Stellan was weeping too. He finally climbed out of the crevasse into the night, into the wind and the starlight that showered down on the just-greening land of the Firth of Uthermere on Stormfast Island.

CHAPTER 20

A Portal Opens

Svenna had kept her promise to the gillygaskins. She returned often to tell them stories. To try to describe the great beauty of the ahalikki, and the magic of dancing with one's mum under the showering light of a rainbow in the night.

"And so the little cubs who simply could not keep still did sit quietly at last. They waited . . . and waited . . . and waited . . . but still no seal came to the breathing hole. They were just about to give up when suddenly . . ."

"A seal came?" Juuls asked.

"No, not a seal," Svenna said to the dozens of little gilly-gaskins gathered around her like a rusty haze. "Something better. The night skies began to flinch with color. A radiance swept the sky. Flowing rivers of colorful light streamed through the darkness. The colors grew brighter and the whole world shimmered. The cubs and their mother, who were very hungry, no longer felt hungry at all. They tipped up their heads and seemed to drink in the light. It was the ahalikki, the lights from the north. And she and her cubs began to dance on the ice floe as the mother sang the Song of the Lights."

"What song?" a little gilly called No Paws asked.

"Let's see if I can remember it. It's been so long since I sang it to my own cubs.

Deep in the winter sky,
At the edge of night,
Like a secret whisper from Urs'lana,
Sing flowers made of light.
These are the colors of our world.
When evening comes to stay,
In folds of night they roil and swirl,
Then vanish the next day.
So come dance with me, my cubs,
Fill your bellies with this light.
It will feed and make you grow.
It's the sky's milk for this night.

The head of another gilly called Abby floated up and nestled on Svenna's shoulder again.

"So did they dance?"

"Oh yes, of course, and their white fur was drenched in the colors of the lights. Some were pink, some palest blue like a summer sky, some green in the glow of the night . . . rainbows come down to earth!" She laughed ruefully. "The cubs were like tiny rainbows bouncing about on floes of ice." The gillys giggled.

Abby pressed her muzzle close to Svenna's ears. "Did . . . did you dance with your cubs in the once-upon-a-time?"

Svenna patted the little floating head and murmured, "I did, Abby! I did!" She felt a little stitch in her heart. *Oh . . . oh . . . yes . . . we danced. How we danced!* A tear squeezed from her eye.

"One more story, please? A Ki-hi-ru, a shape-shifter story?" asked another gilly who had no paws.

"A fox story! Please, please," they all cried.

"The one about the fox who married a bear," said another.

She sighed. "Just one more, cubs." They seemed to shimmer as she addressed them. No one had ever called them cubs, just Tick Tocks.

Svenna knew that in some mysterious way the gillys were becoming whole. They had been cut, maimed, and were still missing limbs from their terrible ordeals on the escapement wheel, but they seemed somehow less broken. The stories were mending them. The tales were beginning to lodge in their souls.

"Once upon a time, there was a beautiful fox. And as you know, the fur of a Nunquivik fox is many times whiter and silkier than that of a bear. And as I have told you, foxes follow the hunting bears and pick up the scraps of seal that the bears don't eat. But this fox had fallen in love with the bear she had been following. She was so in love, but the bear hardly paid attention to her. *I might as well be air,* the fox thought."

"But she wasn't air," one little gilly chuckled. "She's going to turn into —"

"Shush, Birte. Let Svenna tell the story," Juuls admonished the gilly. The gillys loved these Ki-hi-ru stories. Svenna guessed it was because of the magic of changing shapes. In the stories, a creature could actually change its body, and that, of course, was what these gillys desperately wanted to do. Now, as she was concluding the story, she detected a restlessness in the gillys gathered round her. Something was happening.

She felt a riffle of a wind, another thing she had never felt in this tunnel of quivik before. She was suddenly fearful. Had she been found out? Discovered by the Gilraan? She put her paw up to her shoulder, where Abby's head had been seconds before. She blinked as she saw the head floating near her. A port in the ice ceiling of quivik had suddenly opened up, and a breeze blew through softly. She could see the Great Ursus constellation.

"Look!" Juuls cried out. "The sky. We have never seen the sky!"

Then Abby, a very wise cub, wise beyond her scant year of life, whispered, "Does this mean Ursulana is . . . is . . . just out there?"

"I believe it does!" Svenna said, her voice trembling. "I believe it does."

One by one at first, then two by two, and suddenly countless little gillys began to float through the opening in the ice ceiling.

Shadows! Svenna thought. *They have shadows! They are*

mending. Their shadows were spreading across the ice floor as they rose into the starry night. They were growing whole before Svenna's eyes. Abby's head settled on a body that could have only been hers. Juuls was the last to go, and with his paw — not a new paw, but the one he had been born with — he began to wave at Svenna. "Look, I have a shadow now. My spirit shadow!"

"You are on the spirit trail to Ursulana!" Svenna called out, and all the gillys began to scamper and somersault across the night sky on their way. Soon they were clambering up the star ladder to Ursulana. They felt whole, and like little cubs released at last from the nursing den, they could not wait to play in the light of the stars and cast their shadows across the vast ice sea of Nunquivik.

❧

When Svenna arrived at the panel, she listened carefully through the ice to see if the Mystress of the Chimes was in the harmonics lab. But there was only silence. A slight push of the panel and she was back.

She took up some calculations and heard the Mystress entering the main den after going to her dressing chamber.

"Are you still calculating?" she called into the lab.

"Just finished, Mystress."

"Good. I don't have time to take my jewels to the dressing chamber. Do so."

"Yes, Mystress."

"There was an emergency meeting in the Stellata and now another in the lower chamber, but jewels are not required. So put them back for me."

"Yes, as you say, Mystress."

Svenna heard her leave and went out to the main den, where she had left her coronet and earrings on top of the ceremonial sash that designated a Gilraan member. Svenna had a sudden urge to spit on that sash but restrained herself. She vowed not to waste one bit of energy on anger. She was determined to escape. The gillygaskins were free now, free on their way to Ursulana, but she would live — live to see her own cubs again. Carefully picking up the jewels, she took them into the dressing room.

As she entered she stopped short, nearly skidding, which is rare for a bear of the ice country. Seal's blood was splashed on the isinglass mirror. *So the rumor is true — she drinks seal's blood, bathes in seal's blood, to keep her coat lustrous.*

Then the beautiful reflection of Galilya, Mystress of the Chimes, appeared in the mirror next to Svenna's. A smirk spread across her face.

"Forgot to clean up after my beauty routine. Such a rush." She sighed. "Does it disturb you?" Svenna remained silent, too stupefied to answer. "Let's not get all high and mighty. You've never eaten seal before?"

"Is it a pup's blood?"

"And if it is? So what? Clean it up!" She flung the cloth at Svenna.

CHAPTER 21

A Familiar Scent

In a sparse wood in Uthermere, the four cubs, their paws slick with ice, their eyes streaming tears, stood silently, looking up at the sky. It was as if they were drinking the stars. They could not get enough of this night, or the gentle breeze, or the scent of earth unlocked from winter's grip. And yet they were awash in grief and a swirl of other emotions. If felt somehow wrong that they were still alive while Knute had died — for them. Stellan sensed that Jytte, her eyes on the stars, was imagining the beautiful webs the courageous spider had spun for them. She was wondering if that ladder could somehow magically climb all the way to Ursulana — *or what did the spiders call their heaven?*

"I don't know," Stellan whispered into the night, for he had plucked the words right out of his sister's mind.

"Don't know what?" Froya asked. For neither she nor Third knew what Stellan had plucked from Jytte's mind.

"Ursulana," Stellan replied. "What might the spiders call their heaven?"

"Oh," Froya said softly. "Surely Knute will go there. I mean, he died for us. Knute gave up all his silk to save us, and died."

The four cubs kept their heads tipped toward the sky, searching for a beautiful silken thread that would stretch from the earth to the stars above.

Finally, they walked on. Their grief followed them but felt less crushing as they continued to revel in the wonders of this night and this new country.

The tree grew more thickly as they walked farther from Pleek's Plonk. In the Nunquivik, the land never completely thawed, even in summer. The color green was rare, and they had never seen a tree with leaves. But here everything was different. The ground felt spongy at times. They ate sweet sedges and grasses. There were abundant streams with leaping silvery fish. But that wasn't enough to keep Jytte from worrying. How would they find their father? There were no frost spiders to guide them now. How big was this land, this region called Uthermere?

On that first night, they fell asleep beneath a great sprawling tree. Above them the leafy branches spread against the night and the moonlight seeped down like a silver rain. They were reluctant to close their eyes for losing the marvel of it all. And yet neither Stellan nor Jytte could banish the thought of the hideous black ice cells where their father had been tortured. Had he escaped? How had he suffered? And how would they find him here . . . if he was here? They decided that they would first find their way to the banks of the firth and then follow it. It seemed as good a starting place as any. Bears needed to be in dens near water for fish in the summer and seals in the winter when the firths froze.

They had been traveling up the shoreline of the firth for two or three days when Jytte noticed a tree on a high bank that looked different from the others they had seen. She scrambled up the bank.

"What is it?" Stellan called out.

"It's . . . it's a tree with no bark. It's been rubbed." Jytte's eyes were bright with wonder and delight. "Do you remember, Stellan?"

"Remember what?"

"Mum always said that one of the nicest things about these Northern Kingdoms of Ga'Hoole was that there were so many trees — not just for owls but for bears to —"

"Rub against! She called it spring cleaning!"

"Spring-cleaning their pelts," Jytte said gleefully. "It gets the lice and the wood ticks out."

Froya and Third looked on.

"You mean," said Third, "there might be bears around here?"

"Yes, and probably not Roguers. Roguers wouldn't know trees. No trees in the Nunquivik," Stellan said.

"So maybe it's . . . it's Da?" Jytte said hesitantly.

Stellan bolted toward the tree. There was a long bare patch of the tree's trunk exposed, and at the base of the tree was a small mound of shredded bark. "A bear did this, definitely," he announced.

"Look, here's another," Jytte said.

"And another!" Third stood a short distance away, examining a small tree.

"This must be bear country," Jytte said, turning her head slowly.

They walked on, their excitement growing each time they spotted similarly scraped trees. Jytte bounded ahead, always in the lead. It was as if she were expecting to find their father around every bend. She stopped at one very tall tree and tipped her head back, peering up at the top. "You remember how Mum told us that bears in the Northern Kingdoms can climb trees?"

"Really?" Third asked. Again he felt envious. The cubs' mother had taught them so many things, and Taaka had taught Froya and Third nothing.

"Yes," Jytte replied. "Of course, in the Nunquivik, the trees weren't tall enough to climb. Just teensy little things. We would have broken them — even as cubs."

Stellan stopped at the tree. "You know what else you can do with a tree beside climb it?"

"What?" Jytte asked.

"See how thick the bark is on that tree?" He didn't wait for an answer but backed up against the tree and began to rub his back, then his hindquarters.

"What are you doing wiggling your butt like that?" Jytte asked. "Is this some sort of new dance?" She giggled, thinking of how they used to dance with their mum under their ahalikki lights. "A tree dance?"

"No. This feels great! You know how my toothwalker scar sometimes itches? This is how I can scratch it."

The three other cubs began to back up to trees and rub their haunches, backs, and shoulders. They did this for several minutes and then, somewhat refreshed, continued on their journey.

The sun was just setting when Jytte stopped abruptly. Her nose twitched.

Stellan's heart lurched. He knew instantly that something powerful had invaded Jytte's mind. It wasn't words, and not exactly a thought, but more like a . . . scent? How could that be? He had never really riddled a scent that was not on the ground.

He and Jytte both looked at each other.

"It can't be!"

"But it is, Stellan."

"A scent like . . . like . . . Mum?" Stellan asked.

"Not exactly."

Somehow this scent was something they knew as well as their mum, but not quite. It was as if they were both playing tag with a scent. It drew them, reeled them in — or so it seemed — on an invisible thread as powerful as Knute's strongest silk. Straight ahead was a tree. An immense patch had been rubbed bare. Both cubs began to run toward the trunk. Flinging their arms around the tree, they inhaled deeply an aroma as comforting as their mother's milk yet not their mother's milk.

Then from behind the tree came an enormous roar. A fierce sound that shook the forest. Froya and Third froze to the ground, but Stellan and Jytte smashed their faces against the tree they had been embracing, clamped their eyes shut, and tried to bury themselves into the very trunk of the tree. Jytte felt torn in two. She was frightened and yet desperate to see the source of this roar. If she turned around, might it be her father or might it be a Roguer? And when she finally could not wait another second, she turned around and saw a terrible sight.

CHAPTER 22

A Terrible Trick?

It can't be! That was Stellan's first thought. Before them was a grotesque, staggering wreckage of a bear — earless, with old blood and dirt stuck to his fur, and missing three claws on one paw. Could he actually be their father? He was filthy and stank, and yet there was this other scent that they knew so well.

Trembling, Jytte stepped toward him. "D-D-D-D . . . Da?" When he didn't reply, she swallowed and said, "Are you Svern?"

"What do you want?" he snapped.

Jytte blinked rapidly, as if she were not seeing the right bear. As if some terrible trick had been played on her and another bear would surely appear. "You're our father, our da."

"Whatever gave you that idea?" His voice was weak and raspy but at the same time frightening. "Now get out of my territory. I've marked this tree. I've marked it. My territory, you hear me?" Stellan felt every guard hair on his body bristle up. He glanced at Jytte. It was as if she were crumbling from within. Another two seconds and she would be dust on the forest floor.

"We're your cubs," Jytte said in a small voice Stellan didn't recognize.

"You're clearly confused. I suggest you move along."

Jytte seemed to shrink inside her own pelt. She raised a paw as if to ask a question but then dropped it. Stellan felt her desperation as she stood in front of their father, begging him to recognize her. Her mind was black, black as a starless night. Impenetrable. He could read nothing of her thoughts.

He had to do something. He couldn't watch his sister suffer like this. Stellan stepped forward. The top of the bear's head on either side was mutilated. Black skin bubbled up where ears had been. Yet even without his ears, Stellan realized that he himself looked exactly like this bear — his father!

The shape of his head, the slight tilt of his eyes. Once, so long ago, Stellan had peered at his own reflection in the still black water of a pond in summer. It was the time of Dying Ice Moons and his mum had come and stood beside him. "You are the very image of your father, Stellan." And she had been right.

"Sir," he began carefully. "We . . . we have been searching for you."

"I didn't ask to be found."

"You must listen," Stellan said sternly. He felt a fury building in him. He was angry not for his sake but Jytte's.

"I must?" he snarled. "I must do nothing. Now get out of my territory."

Stellan took a deep breath. "We are your territory!"

"Ridiculous!"

Stellan took a step closer. "You stink, but there's another smell beneath the stink."

"And pray what might that be?"

"The scent of our father. It came with our mother's milk. We've come to find you." The bear looked at him. *He notices my ears*, Stellan thought. So he wiggled them a bit.

"You're making fun of me. Of my ears, or what's left of them."

"They were like my ears and you know it." Stellan fought to keep his voice steady, but he was roiling with anger.

A hush fell upon the forest. There was not a twitter from a bird, nor the rustling of a leaf. It was as if the entire forest was holding its breath and waiting. The huge bear wavered a bit, then plopped down. He buried his head between his knees.

"I have no cubs," he muttered. But was there a tinge of shame in his voice. Stellan tried to riddle the bear's thoughts. But it was as if a wall, an impenetrable ice wall, had dropped down.

Jytte was still trembling, but nevertheless she had crept up and tried to pat his shoulder. "You do."

"Don't touch me, bear!"

"We are your cubs and the cubs of Svenna," Stellan replied evenly.

"I have no cubs," Svern bellowed.

"You have me!" Jytte pleaded, and stomped her foot. "You are our father. You cannot say no. You are! You are! You are!" And each time she said the two words, she stomped her foot harder.

Svern lifted a massive paw. *He can't. He wouldn't!* Stellan thought. The paw swung. Jytte screamed but dodged it and bolted into the woods.

"You . . . you . . . disgusting . . . foul . . . ," Stellan sputtered. He could not even bring himself to think of this stinking heap as a bear. Svern blinked. He appeared slightly stunned. In a split second Stellan knew that Svern himself had riddled his own mind. Seen what he looked like in his son's eyes. The bear roared in a terrible kind of agony, then tore off into the woods. No one said a word. It was as if they had been struck dumb by the rage of this bear. Then Stellan looked around.

"Where's Jytte?"

"She was here just a second ago," Froya said.

"Jytte . . . ," Stellan called out. There was no answer. "Jytte!" he wailed into the night.

"Jytte!" they all began calling.

Panic seized Stellan. He knew that his sister's world had just collapsed. The search for Svern had nurtured Jytte through the worst of times.

"All right, we have to find Jytte. Third, you go that way." He pointed in the direction of a fallen tree. "Froya, you go the other direction. I'll go straight ahead. If we find her, we'll meet back here." He paused. "No! Not here." He cast a poisonous glance toward the woods where Svern had disappeared. "Remember that uprooted giant tree we saw earlier?"

Third and Froya nodded.

"Good, we'll meet there."

"But what if we don't find her?" Froya asked.

Fear flashed through Stellan like a sudden flood. He felt as if he might be drowning, drowning in terror of losing his sister. They simply had to find Jytte. Jytte was his world. There was no world without Jytte. His muzzle trembled. Then he glared at Froya. "We'll find her. We will. Don't say that." All the ferocity had vanished. It was as if he were almost pleading with the cub. He tipped his head up. "We'll meet after the Svree star has faded and the morning star rises."

⚜

Jytte ran blindly into the forest. She didn't care where she went. She just wanted to be away — away from that terrible bear. Branches lashed out against her face. The pounding of her own heart thundered in her ears. She wished her heart would burst. She wished she would die. There was nothing, absolutely nothing to live for. She ran and she ran and she ran. She had never run so far and for so long in her life. But she didn't want to stop and she didn't until, as darkness fell, she stumbled on the enormous roots of a tree. She was exhausted and disoriented. She lay there for several minutes, trying to recover her breath but soon fell into a deep and dreamless sleep.

The morning star had risen and then dissolved into the morning light when the three cubs met back at the upturned tree root, weary from their night's hunt for Jytte. Stellan looked ragged and distraught. He barely spoke, but after a brief rest, they all staggered off in new directions. The cubs were careful to plot out their routes so as not to simply retrace their former paths. But there was no sign of Jytte. How could she have vanished so completely?

After several hours, a peculiar and alarming scent began to drift into Jytte's mind. Her nose wrinkled and the scent became stronger as the wind shifted. *Skunk bear!* This was no dream. And yet she was far from that lodge on the banks of the firth where they had spent the night after fleeing the cave. She opened her eyes slowly. Through a thicket of scrub bushes, she saw a bristly angry face peeking out, peering at her, its long fangs bared. She knew what this beast could do. Within a split second the skunk bear sprang from the bush and charged. Without thinking, Jytte leaped up and reached for the lowest branch, swinging herself into the tree. But the skunk bear was right beneath her, his long, slender claws black and glistening. She was not sure what possessed her, but she swung herself upside down on the branch to swing her paw at him. She felt something tear across her face, but then brought her teeth down with all her might on his paw. Blood spurted and she realized that she had a claw clenched in her teeth! A claw and nothing else. The skunk bear was yowling on the ground. A pool of blood was forming around his paw.

Quickly, Jytte reached for the next branch. Her face ran with blood, both her own and that of the skunk bear's, whose claw she still gripped with her teeth. This next branch was slim. It swung mightily with her weight. If it broke, she was done for. She could hear the skunk bear still howling in his rage. She edged closer to the trunk of the tree. If she could just reach the trunk, she could grasp it and hold on.

She heard a crack, and just as the branch broke, Jytte sprang for the trunk, wrapping her arms and her legs around it. Looking down, she saw the creature growing more furious. He was now charging the tree, bashing it with his head and waving his mutilated paw. But the tree barely shook. The trunk was thick and sturdy.

Good! Knock your brains out, Jytte thought. She looked up. If she climbed straight up, she might find a stronger branch she could perch on and wait the beast out. She dug her hind claws in and then pushed while reaching with her front claws and hoisted herself higher. Directly above her head, she saw a broad limb branching off from the trunk. If she could reach that, she would be safe — not just safe, but it might offer a place to rest, for it looked as if another limb joined it from the other side of the tree. It could be a "settle." That's what their mum called a shallow den on the jumble ice when they went out to hunt. A settle was not a true den, just a resting place sheltered from wind or harsh weather.

It was, in fact, a settle, and a comfortable one at that. She could rest with her back against the trunk, one leg dangling over the slightly lower limb and her arm wrapped around the upper one. She could tell that the skunk bear was growing tired. By the time the night began to shred into the gray of dawn, the creature had lumbered off. But Jytte would wait, as he might still be lurking in the thick surrounding brush.

She would wait and think about that awful bear — *Svern, my so-called father.* How could he have led anything? A rebellion of noble bears? Impossible. Had their mum lied to them about their father? The sound of that ragged voice bellowing, *My territory,* still rang in Jytte's ears. She had had to flee. She had no other choice. But she wondered if Stellan had fled too. If he had, would they find each other again? *Of course we will,* she told herself. *Of course.* And yet a thread of doubt crept through her mind. She felt trapped now in this tree — trapped between two monsters — a skunk bear and a mad bear called Svern.

Froya was making her way back to the meeting spot. It made no sense to her that Jytte would run away from a brother who treasured her, and Jytte had always treasured Stellan. If anything, Svern's cruelties should bring Jytte closer to Stellan, for all they had now was each other.

From high above in a treetop, Froya heard a noise. It was a snuffling sound, yet familiar. *Of course,* she thought, *it's a cub weeping.* If there was one thing Froya knew, it was that sound. She had heard Third's weeping, and before Third, she had heard Stellan and Jytte's weeping in the den of Taaka.

But this was impossible. *Cubs don't climb trees. Of course,* she reasoned, *there are no trees in the Nunquivik. But here!*

"Jytte!" Froya tipped back her head. "Jytte, is that you up there?" A broken sob seemed to tumble down the tree. "Jytte, that is you. Why'd you go up there?" Froya heard a deep sigh. But Jytte still said nothing.

How would she explain it to Froya? Of course there was the skunk bear, but so much more. She began to realize that it was not just the loss of her father that troubled her but the shame — the shame of having such a father.

"Skunk bear." That was the easier explanation and a true one.

"A skunk bear attacked you?" Froya's voice was filled with dismay. "Are you sure?"

"What do you mean, sure? Believe me, I've tangled with those beasts before."

"But this time?"

"I bit off his claw before he could grab me," Jytte replied curtly.

"You what?" Froya gasped.

"Bit off his claw. That's why he couldn't follow me up this

tree. They have long, sharp, hooked claws. Without it he had no chance of climbing up after me."

"That's incredible." Froya cocked her head.

"I have the claw to prove it."

An idea came to Froya. "I don't believe you," she snapped.

"It's true!"

"Show me," Froya said. "Come down and show me." Her voice was quarrelsome. Jytte had never heard this tone coming from the normally meek Froya.

"Oh sure, very clever, Froya."

"Well, how long are you planning on staying up there?" she sneered.

"None of your business."

This angered Froya. "No, Jytte. It is my business. If you're not coming down, I'm coming up."

And with that she began to climb. It was easier than she had thought. She arrived just beneath the branch where Jytte was perched.

She gasped at the sight of Jytte's face. There was a wound that sliced across her cheek, raw and still oozing blood from the black torn skin. "You look awful!"

"You would too!" She held up a long, curved black claw.

Froya swallowed. It was a fearsome-looking thing. "Lucky it wasn't your eye."

"Too bad it wasn't my heart." She closed her eyes tight. It was as if she could feel the jagged edges of her own torn heart.

"You want to die?" Froya almost gasped as she said the words. This seemed unbelievable. After all they had gone through, Jytte would choose to die!

Jytte lifted her paws to her face and began to cry.

"Jytte, why did you run away?"

"I . . . I have nothing left."

"Nonsense." Froya reached up and patted her knee that was hanging down from the limb just above her head. "You have Stellan. Stellan is lost without you."

"But I am lost without my father. My father is a fake, a fraud. Our mum must have lied about him." She felt stupid and ashamed. Why had she had these hopes, these dreams? But she had, and there was nobody who could really understand her — not even Stellan. To let go of a dream was the hardest thing in life.

"You are lost without the father you created in your mind. That father never existed," Froya said. She tried to keep her voice steady, but she felt Jytte's anguish so deeply.

"But you said he existed. You said he was the leader of the rebellion, a hero."

"He could be all that and not a good father. My mum, Taaka, was a terrible, vicious mother and nothing else."

Jytte sniffled. "Well, still."

"Well, still what?" Froya pressed.

"Nothing," Jytte said stubbornly.

"You're wrong, Jytte. So wrong." She shook her head. "There is something. The mission. The Den of Forever Frost."

She spoke with great determination. "Listen to me. There is still the Ice Clock to stop and cubs to be saved."

"Without our father, there is no hope for finding that den."

"Come back with me, Jytte. Your brother is suffering. Stellan has lost a father and now you. Maybe your father didn't have a choice, but you do. Come back."

"What choice is there now?"

Froya stretched up so that she was almost level with the limb on which Jytte was perched.

"What do you mean, what choice is there? There is a world out there, Jytte, and it is waiting for you."

Hesitantly Jytte began to climb down the tree.

CHAPTER 23

"We're Your Brats!"

Stellan blinked as he saw the two approaching. Could it be? Relief began to flood through him. It was his sister, and she looked unharmed except for the dried blood on her face.

"Jytte!" Stellan shouted, racing toward her. The two cubs embraced and tumbled to the ground.

"I'm sorry, I'm sorry. I . . . I . . . ," Jytte sobbed as they picked themselves up. "I never should've run away."

"Oh, Jytte, what happened to your face?"

She touched it lightly. A scab was forming. A black scab, she thought, just like the bubbling black skin where her father's ears had been. *Father, I cannot call him Father.* He was just a shattered dream now.

"A skunk bear clawed me." She tried to sound brave.

"A skunk bear?"

"Yes. I climbed a tree and escaped." She spoke nonchalantly, as if this were an everyday occurrence. She could appear as if what had happened had not damaged her or wounded her. The last thing she wanted was their pity as she stood in the shards of her fractured dream.

"You climbed a tree!" Stellan gasped. He had never heard of a bear climbing a tree.

"A tree?" Third asked. "A real tree?"

"Yes, a real tree and a real skunk bear." She was looking about on the ground.

But now Jytte began to quaver a bit. How long could she pretend? She took a deep breath. "I'm sorry I left you. I was just so . . . so . . . I mean, I can't believe that bear was our father. I was such a fool."

Stellan saw her struggling to pretend that she was fine, fine and brave and undiminished by her father's cruelty. Gently, Stellan put his arm around her shoulders. "Come along, sister. There's a stream below. I think there are some fish."

"And there are plump berries too," Third said. "Much fatter and juicier than the ones in the Nunquivik. We need to eat and rest."

The days had grown longer, so they were able to fish and find berries well into the night. The four cubs sat together on the banks of the stream covered with thick moss. Stellan could feel the remnants of Jytte's grief swirling through her mind.

She had made a valiant effort to appear strong, but in the deepest recesses of her mind he sensed the pieces of that shattered dream. They lurked like ghosts, gillygaskins that could not ascend to Ursulana. He tried all sorts of subjects to distract her.

"Mum told us once," Stellan began, "that the owls used this moss in their hollows. It made the softest of beds for their hatchlings."

"Hatch-whats?" Froya said. "What are those?"

"Baby owls," Jytte said. "They hatch out of eggs. They aren't born the way we are. Not exactly."

"Very mysterious, the ways of other creatures," Third said.

"Very mysterious, the ways of our father," Jytte muttered to herself.

"Your mum taught you so much," Froya said. "About owls, about the language spoken here — Krakish — about the star Nevermoves."

"And our father taught us nothing," Jytte said bitterly. "I never want to see him again."

Stellan shook his head. "No," he said firmly. "What you need to do . . . what we need to do is to confront him. Demand an explanation and tell him of our mission. And that we need his help because Mum was captured by Roguers." Stellan paused. "What do you say, Jytte? You have never in your life dodged a fight. You have a scar down your cheek from a skunk bear. I have one on my haunch from a toothwalker. How much damage can a fake father do? And the least we can do is tell him who we are. Show him who we are. We have to find him. He can't have gone far. He was weak."

"He was a wreck," Jytte said bitterly.

Jytte had grown very still as she looked at her brother. Perhaps Stellan was right. Forget who *he* is. Tell Svern who *they* are. Challenge him not to be a father but a fellow rebel. A teacher.

She nodded. "All right, let's go find him."

Tracking Svern was hardly challenging. His footsteps were distinctive — wobbly, uncertain, and oftentimes he seemed to go in circles. They heard him before they saw him, propped against a tree trunk, snoring loudly. The cubs stopped and stared at him for a moment as he slept, oblivious to their presence

Despite his large size, Stellan realized that his father was painfully thin. His bones seemed to almost poke through his pelt. Third and Froya felt Stellan's and Jytte's pain at seeing the wreckage of this once-noble bear. Svern's eyelids began to twitch, and within a few seconds he was awake. But his breathing was labored. What had they done to him in that black ice ort?

Stellan turned to Third and Froya. "Go get some fish. The fat silvery ones with the pink flesh," he ordered.

"Is he dying, Stellan?" Jytte asked.

"No. He's just weak . . . weak from the black ice ort." He hoped this was true.

Jytte and Stellan sat down in front of Svern and waited patiently. He began to stir ever so slightly.

"You still here?" The cubs nodded. "I thought it was a bad dream. But I wake up and here you are."

"We're not a dream, any kind of dream. We're real and we're here. We plan to stay," Jytte said defiantly.

Stellan wanted to caution his sister. He'd glimpsed their father's thoughts and realized that, in his head, this wreckage of a once-honorable bear was actually crying. Deeply, silently, secretly, he was weeping with shame and regret.

"Why do you want to stay?" he croaked hoarsely.

"We're your cubs," Stellan said matter-of-factly. "And we need your help."

"Don't you know that it's unnatural for cubs to stay with their father, even if I was your father?"

"Not if our mum is gone. Captured by Roguers," Jytte said.

Svern's broad chest seemed to sink into his frail body. "No, no . . . ," he muttered weakly.

"But you're here. You're our father," Jytte said firmly. The grit in Jytte's voice seemed to kindle something in Svern. His dull black eyes flickered.

"You're a couple of sassy little brats, aren't you?" But all the rage had vanished from his voice.

"We're your brats and Svenna's." Jytte paused. "You're Svern." The sound of his own name being spoken sent a shudder through him.

"But it's not the custom for father bears to be with cubs."

Stellan glanced at his sister. The words *custom* or *customary* always set her off.

Jytte leaned over close to the bubbly nubbins that had once been his ears. She felt as though her heart was breaking. "Da, I don't like the word 'custom.' Now listen to me. Does the name Skagen mean anything to you?"

Svern was suddenly alert. "It does, but how do you know about him?"

"Skagen taught us," Stellan said.

"Skagen! Skagen the snow leopard taught you? Taught you what?" The questions came in a rush. Stellan was startled. He didn't think his father had enough breath in his frail body to ask such a stream of questions. Svern now scratched his head, as if he were slightly confused about what Stellan had told them.

Stellan nodded at Jytte as if to encourage her to speak up, to say something.

Jytte began speaking very slowly. She wanted him to understand every word. Svern's eyes rested on her attentively. A tiny flicker of hope fluttered in her mind. "Skagen taught us about the Den of Forever Frost." She paused. She dared not call him Father but she had been tempted, as he seemed much more sensible now. "And he taught us about you. That you were the leader of the rebellion."

"I led nothing." Svern's voice cracked.

"You did," Jytte said firmly. "You did, and you know how to break the clock. Skagen said that's the only way to free the bears at the Ice Cap."

"I tried, but I didn't have the key. You need a key to stop the gears. And there's no way to get the key, I fear. It's been lost for centuries in the Den of Forever Frost."

"How did it get there?" Stellan asked.

"I honestly don't know how it got there. It could have been an accident of nature. Earthquakes followed the Great Melting. Things were lost, rearranged. Glaciers slid, continents were broken. Mountain ranges sank. Everything was scrambled."

"We should go look for it!" Jytte said, thrilled by the prospect of an adventure with her father.

Svern shook his head. "The Den of Forever Frost is protected by an ice maze. No one ever speaks of that, but it's impossible to get through."

"No it's not!" Stellan said. There was a sharpness in Stellan's voice that snagged Svern's attention.

"Are you defying me, young cub?"

Stellan looked straight at his father. "The Bear Council used to meet in the Den of Forever Frost, so it *must* be possible to make it through the maze. We have to try."

Svern glared at his son, but a moment later the glare dissolved, leaving only a misty sad light in his eyes. "Yes, the Bear Council knew the way through the maze, but that knowledge has been lost for generations. Believe me, I've tried. It's hopeless."

"We have to try again." Stellan paused. "You see, Da —"

A current passed through Jytte. She could hardly believe that Stellan had dared call Svern Da. Stellan continued, "Our mum is a prisoner of the clock, and so are countless little cubs.

Svern seemed to sag. His pelt drooped and the black bubbled scars on top of his head had begun to twitch. "Stellan, you really think that? That they have Svenna at the Ice Clock?"

. "Yes, Da," Stellan said. Svern turned toward Jytte. She nodded solemnly in agreement.

He shook his head in disbelief, then turned and looked at both his children. "But whatever gave you the idea that *you* could stop this infernal clock?"

"Skagen," the two cubs answered at once.

"Skagen? You really found Skagen. He is a creature of great stealth."

"He actually found us," Stellan said.

"How? The creature is a recluse. He seeks no company. No friends."

"We weren't looking for him. That's for sure," Jytte said. "We kind of just stumbled across him. His cave, that is."

"And then?" Svern asked.

"We lived with Skagen," Stellan said. "Lived with him until the Roguers killed him."

"They killed him?" Tears began to form in their father's eyes.

"Yes," Jytte replied softly. "Skagen is dead."

"And Skagen said you could do this? Break the clock?" Svern asked.

"He said we could try," Stellan answered.

At this moment, Froya and Third came back with some fish, which Jytte tore apart and passed to her father. He seemed to regain some strength as he started eating.

"So, young'uns, you said you don't like the word 'custom'? Too bad." Even though the fight had gone out of his voice, it irritated Jytte.

"Yes." Jytte tossed her head. "Most customs are ridiculous. Like fathers abandoning their cubs, for example."

"I didn't abandon you. I left you with the best she-bear in all the Northern Kingdoms. And let me tell you, cubs, your mother, Svenna, is a noble bear. The noblest of bears." Stellan could almost feel, or see in his mind, Svern's breaking heart.

"So help us find her," Jytte said softly. "Skagen told us that you're a hero."

"I am no hero. I was caught. I was tortured. But I got away somehow." He paused and buried his face in his paws. "I fled, but I left a good bear, my partner, Nicco, behind in order to save my own life."

"It's not your fault," Jytte said softly.

"Well, who else's fault would it be?" he growled and gave her a sorrowful look. Then, groaning, he touched the scabs on his head. They had begun to ooze a dark liquid. He growled, picked a flask off the ground, and tipped it back.

Svern's eyes seemed to swim in their sockets. He blinked once, twice, three times, and then fell over softly onto his side and within seconds was snoring loudly.

The cubs looked at one another in alarm.

"He hardly ate any of the fish," Froya said.

"But he did take several swallows of this stuff," Stellan said, picking up the flask and sniffing it. He began pouring it out onto the ground.

"Stellan, Da probably needs that for his ears. For the pain."

"He needs food," Stellan said firmly. "Let's look for some honeyfrost. That will do his ears a lot more good." Stellan stood up and flung the empty flask into a thick stand of brush.

CHAPTER 24

A Code Discovered

Svenna rushed toward the Oscillaria with a set of calculations. The Mystress had presented them to her that morning and asked that Svenna take them to Master Udo immediately.

The Master of the Pendulum and the Mystress of the Chimes worked together closely, for they both focused their mathematical calculations on the arc swing of the pendulum of the Ice Clock.

Svenna listened closely as she made her way through the maze of ice corridors. She had learned that sound could be warped or distorted, allowing her to overhear conversations as she had near the Stellata Chamber. She was surprised that no other bears had discovered this peculiarity. Even whispers could be overheard, and she'd begun to think of these places as the whisper bends.

"More defections near the Nunqua ice shelf region." The words of two whispering Roguers seemed to fall directly into her ears.

Nunqua ice shelf, Svenna thought. That was where she and her cubs had come from.

"How's our agent doing there?"

"She's good. A bit impulsive. She's proving better as an administrator than a tracker."

"What about the double agent, Nicco? Didn't he help one of her victims escape?"

"Yes, the Yinqui, but the Roguers got him."

Yinqui . . . like Svern. Panic surged through Svenna, panic with an edge as sharp as a blade. The one who escaped — could it have been Svern? Could he have somehow escaped?

She tried to slow her steps. She wanted to hear more, but the two bears were approaching, and as they came closer, their voices began to fade. They had passed the point that warped sound.

Svenna was so preoccupied that she nearly missed the turn-off for the Oscillaria. She came to a sudden stop by the entrance, which was guarded by a prefect.

"Your purpose?" he barked.

"I'm delivering a set of calculations from the Mystress of the Chimes to Master Udo, Master of the Pendulum."

"I must examine them first."

"They are sealed, sir. Triple sealed."

"Let her through," Master Udo snapped from his seat at a high desk from which he could observe all who came and left the Oscillaria's ice gates. "I'll open the calculations."

Svenna walked up to the high desk and presented the scroll of sealscap to the Master of the Pendulum. He reached down and took them from her with a trembling paw. This struck her as odd, as Master Udo was not an old bear.

"Report to the Mystress of the Chimes that I shall have the final derivations back to her in six hours, twenty-five minutes, fourteen seconds, and three milliseconds."

"Yes, Master Udo." Svenna nodded and withdrew from the Oscillaria.

She returned to the Mystress of the Chimes's apartments and was about to knock on the door to her library, but Svenna stopped short when she heard odd muffled whining sounds. These strange mewling cries were not like any sound a bear would ever make, more like a small wounded animal's. The creature was sobbing. Was it another seal pup giving his blood for the Mystress's lustrous pelt?

Svenna retreated to the receiving den in the Mystress's quarters. A few minutes later, the Mystress came in, crisp, calm, and imperious — her usual demeanor.

"When did you get back?" the Mystress demanded.

"Just three seconds and two milliseconds ago," Svenna lied.

"Good!" Was there a dim light of relief in the bear's tawny eyes? Had she never noticed before how golden the Mystress's eyes really were?

"Yes, ma'am. Master Udo says that he will have the calculations back to you in six hours, twelve minutes, twelve seconds, and two milliseconds."

The Mystress sniffed. "Excellent. Now please scrape the floor in here, as I expect visitors later and I noticed that the ice is rough." She scraped the floor lightly with her foot. "Following that, go to my harmonics lab. There are some final equations that must be prepared for the Grand Patek to review." Without another word, she swept out of the den.

The ice floor in the Mystress's receiving den was indeed quite untidy, and it took Svenna a good while — or one hour, two minutes, and thirty-five seconds — to restore it to the pristine finish that the Mystress's fastidious nature demanded.

Svenna finally made her way to the harmonics lab and took her place on the bench to figure out the calculations. As she took out a fresh piece of sealscap to place on the tablet, she noticed that the marks from the previous calculations that the Mystress had worked on were still visible. This batch of sealscap was especially thin and the impressions from bone sliver used as a marker were often left on the tablet.

"What in the world," she murmured to herself. These were not exactly equations but rather a confusing jumble of mathematical symbols that seemed to signify nothing. Were these the calculations that Svenna had delivered to Master Udo in the Court of the Pendulum?

$$\sqrt{z} = \sqrt{r}\, \exp(i\varphi/2)$$

$$dx = (b^3 - a^3 \in \mathbb{Z}, x \in [0,1 \in \mathbb{Z}, 1\ (A \cap B) \subseteq A \pm {}^3\sqrt{a}\cos = \cong$$

Cube roots danced across the ice with square roots. Cosines mingled with plus and minus symbols in a nonsensical manner. Parentheses were scattered helter-skelter throughout. It began to dawn on Svenna that these were not calculations, not formulas, not equations, but a code! A code through which perhaps she was communicating with Master Udo. Was that what Svenna had delivered to him hours before? What secrets did it hold?

CHAPTER 25

"Me, Teach You?"

Jytte was dabbing honeyfrost on the still-festering wounds of Svern's ears. The cubs stayed by Svern all through the night. He seemed to be in a very deep sleep and yet there were moments when he became agitated, as if seized by terrible nightmares. He finally woke up and cautiously touched his head.

"What's that?" he growled, looking at the goo on his paw.

"Honeyfrost," Jytte said. "I'll put some more on now."

"How about some fish, Da?" Stellan said. "Third and Froya got some nice fish for you. It's down by the shore."

"Won't hurt, I guess." Svern groaned and crawled up onto his knees. It was painful for the cubs to watch their father as he lumbered slowly toward the bank of the river. Stellan had laid the fish out on a flat rock and now began to strip the flesh from it. Svern watched him with interest. "You're parsing that fish nicely, picking out all the small bones for me." He chuckled.

"Feeding me like a cub. Where'd you learn how to strip a fish?"

"Mum," Stellan said without looking up. "She taught us everything. She also told us stories. That's how we know about the Den of Forever Frost."

"You shouldn't waste any more time thinking about that place," Svern said flatly.

Jytte and Stellan were stricken. "Da," Jytte ventured. "We can't just give up. If you're not going to help us, then we'll have to find the key on our own."

"Absolutely not," Svern snapped. "There are things deep in that ice maze."

"What kind of things?" Jytte pressed.

Svern shook his head violently, as if trying to sweep something from his mind. "Nothing you need to know about," he muttered.

Stellan was studying his paws as if they were the most interesting thing in the world. He did not speak for a long time. *He's riddling*, Jytte realized. Her brother was riddling his father's mind for information about those *things*. What scents was Stellan picking up? Why were his nostrils twitching as the edges of his ears quivered?

Svern's thoughts were being parsed, picked over just as Stellan had picked over those fish bones. His father looked up at him suddenly, a new sharpness in his eyes. It frightened Stellan, and he stopped his riddling. He felt ashamed, embarrassed, as if he had seen something he was not supposed to.

"Uh . . . I'll get you some fish, Da."

"You do that," Svern said coldly. Stellan nodded and hurried off.

Jytte sensed that Stellan had riddled his way into dangerous territory in Svern's mind. She wanted to find out what Stellan had seen. She turned to Svern. "I think I'll go help Stellan fish."

Jytte scampered down to the shore, where Stellan was just bringing up a second fish. "What did you riddle, Stellan? What did you see?"

"I saw the key in the Den of Forever Frost, but I also saw frightening things — monsters, glaring ice, ice so bright it burns your eyes . . . and hags, haggish creatures like the ones the frost spiders told us about . . . and . . . and something else that I didn't understand."

"What?" Jytte asked impatiently.

"Something black . . . like a fang."

"A fang? But fangs aren't black, Stellan."

"I know, I can't explain it. But whatever's inside that maze, it's not something a parent would want a cub to think about, let alone face."

"Catch any more fish, young'uns?" Svern called. Jytte felt a tiny glow inside her when he called them young'uns. It seemed right. And now she understood why her father didn't want them looking for the Den of Forever Frost. He wanted to protect them. Svern must love them in his odd, grumpy way.

"These are really fat, Da, fat and tender," Jytte replied. "Take some."

"You cubs are going to spoil me with all this attention." He chuckled.

"Da," Stellan began. "I saw the ice maze you told us about with the glaring ice, and I saw —"

Svern cut him off. "How did you see all this?" he asked, startled.

"Jytte and I have gifts. Jytte is an ice gazer and I'm a riddler."

"A riddler," Svern repeated, his voice full of wonder. "Your great-aunt Svakyn was a riddler. What else did you see?"

"I saw monsters. I also saw the key. The key for stopping the clock. I understand why you think it's too dangerous, but I can find the key. I know I can."

Svern furrowed his brow. The bubbly nubbins where his ears had been seemed to collide. His entire face was knotted in worry. "I can't let you go into the maze alone."

"You could guide us." Jytte reached out and grasped her father's paw.

"Guide you?" Svern said softly. His eyes seemed fixed on some distant horizon.

"Teach us," Jytte said. She felt as if the huge gulf between them was finally closing. They were reaching him in a new way.

"You could, Da, you could teach us!" Stellan saw this in his sister's head. She was right. Something was mending and it was more than his wounds.

"Me, teach you?" A wondrous look filled the old bear's eyes. "Me a, teacher!"

CHAPTER 26

A Team of Sorts

With the aid of the fish and honeyfrost, Svern grew stronger. By the next day, his ears had begun to heal, and he seemed more energetic and alert.

"Da, when are you going to train us to fight those monsters in the Den of Forever Frost?" Jytte asked.

Svern shook his head wearily. "I'm not sure it's worth it. Even if we manage to find the key, there's almost no way of getting to the clock."

"But *you* got close!" Jytte said. "Skagen told us that you nearly succeeded."

"But I didn't suceed." Svern let out a long sigh. "The operation failed. Many were lost — including some very dear friends. It was dangerous to try it, and it is even more dangerous to go into the Den of Forever Frost."

Stellan drew himself up to his full height, which was considerable now. No bear would take him for a mere cub any longer. His tongue had turned blue like a grown-up polar bear's. When he and Jytte were born their tongues were pink. It seemed that at least fifty times a day they would check each other's tongues. But now they were big blue-tongued bears, and Stellan felt they deserved some answers.

"Da, we need to do this. We don't have a choice. We have to try to break the clock and rescue Mum."

"Whether you're willing to help us or not." Jytte said this slowly, not in a voice that begged but one that was absolutely resolved.

"If I allowed you to go, I would be no better than those Timekeepers at the Ice Clock who sacrifice young cubs on the escapement wheel. You would be slaughtered." Svern's voice cracked. "You're too young."

"We're not too young," Jytte said firmly. "Look at us! Our tongues are blue." Jytte and her brother stuck out their tongues to show their father.

Svern chuckled and looked at his cubs. "So you think you're almost grown up, do you, with your blue tongues and all. But are you grown up enough to die? Tell me that."

"It's our destiny, and this is our quest," Jytte said.

"And who told you that bit of nonsense? Skagen, I suppose."

The cubs nodded. Svern stared off into the dim light of the forest. "He told you that this was your destiny?"

"He said our stories await us," Stellan replied.

A distant look came into his eyes. "That is what destinies are in part: untold stories."

"We can do this, Da." Jytte leaned forward. "Remember, I am an ice gazer and Stellan is a riddler."

"And you, I guess, are a dreamwalker?" Svern said, turning to Third.

Third gasped. "How did you guess?"

"I felt you tromping about in my fever dreams. My own mum was one."

Svern turned to Froya. "And what are you?"

"I am nothing. I tried to save my friend from the Roguers, but in truth she saved me and died for it."

Svern reached out and touched Froya's head gently. "You tried, Froya. I never even tried." In that moment, Svern knew that if the cubs went to the Den of Forever Frost, he would have to go with them. This must be their mission together.

"So we have a riddler, a dreamwalker, an ice gazer, and" — he gazed fondly on Froya — "a hero. A team of sorts." He paused and sighed deeply. "Perhaps it is your destiny to enter the Den of Forever Frost and find your way to the key. But it is treacherous now. Stellan, you saw those monsters in my head — the dragon walruses, the hagsfiends." Stellan nodded. "In the time of Great Melting, there were immense earthquakes that rattled the very innards of this land, including the Den of Forever Frost. It was not destroyed, but it was . . . how shall I put it?

Confused, rearranged — discombobulated. The den still exists, but the channels appeared to have been reshuffled. To get there, one has to go through a maze of *klarken* ice."

"We know klarken ice," Jytte said. "You can almost see through it."

"That's exactly the problem. You can see through it to other ice. And it becomes like an endless maze of mirrors. You lose your sense of direction entirely. But not only that — there are other dangers."

"Frost vipers?" Stellan said. "We know about them." He felt almost weak as he recalled the glare of those red eyes advancing on him, the forked tongue lashing out.

"Yes. Their venom means instant death if they break from the slither. But there are creatures worse than frost vipers. You never know when you might come across *hyrakium*."

"What's that?" Jytte asked eagerly as a mixture of fear and excitement coursed through her.

"A death pit for a monstrosity from the past, the very long-ago past."

"Like . . . like a hagsfiend?" Stellan asked, remembering what Akka the frost spider had said about the horrible haggish owls who could spin webs with their eyes to ensnare creatures.

"Yes, those, and dragon walruses as well. The hyrakiums are where the bones for these ancient monsters lie. One must be careful crossing the region. A disturbance can reawaken the monsters."

"They come back to life?" Stellan asked hesitantly. There was a tremor in his voice.

"They stay beneath the earth's crust, but they can gather back their bones. Reassemble them and kill you beneath the earth. Back in the yore, it was much easier for the bears of the council to get to the Den of Forever Frost. There was no ice maze riddled with hyrakiums." Svern paused and looked at the four cubs. "So before you go, you need to be prepared."

"How?" Jytte asked. "How do we prepare?"

"I agreed to be your teacher. In Ga'Hoole they call a teacher a *ryb*. I can become your ryb and teach you the way of the ice sword." There was a kindling in the bear's eyes. "Come along, I'll take you to my den — my winter den."

CHAPTER 27

The Den of Svern

The four cubs stood in amazement as they looked about at the winter den. On the walls hung a variety of diagrams, maps, pictures etched on sealscap, and some odd-looking things made of peculiar materials.

"Da?" Jytte asked. "Have you always lived in this den?"

"More or less," Svern replied. He could be frustratingly vague at times.

Third's eyes settled on a pair of clawlike objects.

"What are those?" Third asked.

"Battle claws first made for the owls. And next to it is a war hammer. I have all manner of weapons here. This is my own private armory. I was a collector at one time."

"Did you use them when you led the rebellion?" Jytte asked. Her eyes were wide with wonder. Stellan could see that she was trying to imagine holding one. Bringing it down on a Roguer bear's head. Fighting off a skunk bear.

"Yes, I used some then, and some before."

"Before what?" Jytte took a step closer to her father.

"I'm fairly old, you know. When I was very young, I helped some of the owls in their skirmishes with their enemies. Helped defeat some very bad owls known as the Pure Ones." He sighed, then said, "Once upon a time."

"Once upon a time," Stellan said. "You talk as if it was a story."

"It was no simple story. It was a war, all right. These wars never seem to end, do they?"

"But these battle claws aren't made of ice," Stellan said.

"Indeed not. Iron. Stronger than the hardest ice — except that from the Ice Dagger in the Everwinter Sea. You know, of course, the first collier came from this region. Grank was his name."

"What's a collier?" Froya asked.

"A collier is a collector of coals. Only owls can do it. They fly over burning forests or even the slopes of volcanoes and collect the red-hot coals."

"What do they do with them?" Stellan asked.

"They take them to the forges of the smithies where they are used to forge metals into this!" Svern suddenly seized a long blade that glittered in the dim light of the den. The cubs gasped as he raised it and held it in the air. There was a magnificence about him as he stood with the blade glowing in the half-light of the den. His pelt, which had been raggedy and stained when they first found him, now glistened. It was as if an entirely different bear was towering before them — earless yet powerful. "This, my friends, is a sword forged in the fires of Bubo, one of the great blacksmiths of Ga'Hoole."

"An owl?" Stellan asked. This was mystifying, trying to imagine a creature creating this weapon with fire.

"Indeed. A great horned with feathers as red as the flames in his forge."

"But it's not ice," Jytte said. "Where's the ice sword you mentioned?" She looked about. Never had she seen such things. Never had she been in such a den. It was all so odd but fascinating, exciting. She imagined herself standing beside her father, wielding these weapons.

"The ice weapons are in my sub-den. Follow me," Svern said, and tipped his head to indicate where he was leading them.

He headed down a winding passageway that he called a *ghyll*. Off the ghyll were other dens, none as large as the first one they had entered.

"This is my armory," he said. The ice walls were hung with all sorts of blades, shields, and even ice helmets. He tapped one of the helmets. "Great camo ops."

"What's that?" Froya asked.

"Camouflage operations. Wear one of these and the enemy thinks you're just another mountain peak in the distance."

"And this?" Froya asked. She took a tiny needle like sliver of ice from a holder on the wall.

"An ice splinter. Very deadly, with good aim. Too tiny, of course, for easy use in the huge paws of a bear, but perfect for the Frost Beak units. It's an elite force of tiny owls, pygmies and elf owls, that we fought alongside in the battle with the Pure Ones in the Northern Kingdoms. Remember I told you we sometimes helped out the owls? But I was also a Yinqui, as you already know. Follow me and I'll show you to my listening nook."

They continued walking and then came to a small, round den not large enough to hold more than a single full-grown bear.

"This nook was the center of my listening operations. Well, let's call it what it is — spying. The nook is actually an old dried-out smee hole."

"I'm not sure I understand what you're talking about. So many new words!" Jytte said. This was such a new world — new words, new strange objects: ice swords and special owls like colliers.

"A steam vent. They dot the entire region here. Over time they dry up as the steam from hot springs or volcanoes finds another course. The walls become sound conductors. Your great-great-many-times-great-grandfather Svarr, mate of Svenka, was a famous Yinqui during the Hag Wars," Svern explained.

"Is that the war the Great Marven fought in?" Stellan asked.

"No. That was not really a war when Marven distinguished himself. Near that time but before the seas had risen and the dragon walruses emerged. Quite a bear, that Marven. No equal as a swimmer.

"Now, cubs, to thread your way through the ice maze of the Den of Forever Frost, you need skills far beyond the ones you already possess. So I suggest that we begin our training with daggers."

"Daggers?" Froya asked, and attempted to disguise the fear in her voice. Would her shoulder be up to using a dagger? She stole a glance at Jytte. Jytte never seemed to fear anything. She was just now dancing about as if sparring with an imaginary opponent. Jytte stopped suddenly and looked at the real dagger Svern held out. "So how do I hold it? My paw? My mouth?" There was a bright eagerness in her eyes.

"Your paw. Sometimes both paws when you attack. Gives you twice the power," Svern replied. He took the dagger in both paws and swung it down. A great draft blew across the cubs' faces, flattening the fur.

"Now follow me to a practice den."

Svern fetched a variety of ice weapons from the passageway. He carried all of these in a whaleskin sling.

"I shall equip each of you with a sling like this, as well as one of these." He drew out a loop of cured sealskin that he slung over his shoulders. "This is called a bandolier. It is a device for carrying ice splinters."

"But I thought only the tiny owls, the Frost Beaks, used those," Third said.

"True, but I had — before my unfortunate events in the Nunquivik — experimented with other methods of launching these splinters. We'll get to that. But first let's try out the ice swords. One begins with the proper grip and stance."

Holding the sword aloft, he turned to the side so he was not facing the cubs squarely. "You never want to face your opponent directly. Do you know why?"

"Uh . . . the enemy could strike you in the face?" Jytte asked.

"Or worse, the heart!" Svern said. "So this is the proper stance. You present less of a target when turned to the side. You then must learn to advance by stepping forward but still turned to the side. So this will be our first lesson." He drew out some slender alder branches.

"We don't get to use real ice swords?" Jytte asked. Her shoulders slumped.

"Not yet. You must become proficient in advancing while holding the sword aloft and in this position. See that twig protruding from the wall? That is my target. Now watch me slice it off."

Svern, with delicate quick steps, advanced on the twig and in one quick swipe sliced it from the wall of the den. "Now, I know what you're thinking. That is not a dragon walrus or a hagsfiend. It's a twig. It's not moving. True. But try doing it with these twigs that I call pegs." He walked up to the wall and stuck in the pegs. "Give it a try, Third."

Third began moving forward with his body turned to the side. His feet became impossibly tangled up, and he fell down.

"This is harder than it looks," Third said. "Urskadamus!" he muttered hotly beneath his breath. Stellan blinked. He had never, as long as he had known Third, heard him say even the mildest curse.

"Can I try the dagger?" Jytte asked. She was almost jumping up and down with excitement.

"Yes, the dagger is for close fighting. You have to use quick upthrust movements like this." Svern demonstrated with a real ice dagger. There was a sharp whistle of air as he brought the dagger up. "Now try it, Jytte."

"This is a real ice dagger . . . not . . . not a pretend one?" she said, the excitement brimming in her voice.

"Try it. You need to accustom yourself to the heft of it. All of you. Just stand apart. If you can make the air whistle, you're doing it right."

The cubs stood a distance apart, and each began practicing the move that Svern had just shown them. Stellan began by holding the dagger and angling himself so that his chest was turned away from his imagined opponent. He raised the blade.

"That's it, Stellan. You might turn a tad bit farther and then begin to advance."

Svern turned his attention to Jytte. "Jytte, your stance is perfect, but not so many big steps. Shorten your steps yet at the same time quicken them, then thrust."

Froya was practicing in a far corner. She was quite determined, though Stellan felt she was a tad nervous at the same time. And just at that moment, Svern complimented her.

"Good, Froya. Very good."

She gave a fragile smile. "Am I holding the dagger high enough?"

"Yes. You don't have to hold it as high as I demonstrated with the long blade. You'll be fighting a lot closer. So indeed you could lower it a bit, then slash sideways."

There was no whistling as there had been when Svern brought the long blade down. The air remained still after several attempts by all the cubs, but suddenly there was a tiny squeak.

"You almost got it, Jytte. Almost. You see what she did, cubs?"

"What did I do?" Jytte looked at her father, perplexed.

"You squatted a bit. It gave more power to your upthrust. Now try it again. Bend your knees. Then pop up."

Froya was shocked when she realized that it was her dagger that produced the next squeak!

"*Utmyrket!*" Svern cried out.

"Huh?" Froya said.

Svern was jubilant. He leaped up a bit, waving his own dagger. "Utmyrket! Splendid — take a bow. That's what it means in old Krakish."

Froya felt a thrill of delight surge through her.

Her brother Third, however, was still struggling.

Svern turned to him. "It's all in the knees, Third. It really does add power."

Surprisingly, Stellan, the largest and strongest of the cubs, was the last to master the dagger and produce a clear whistling sound. But he did it.

"You did it, Stellan! You did it. And though you were last to do it, that was the shrillest of all the whistles," Svern said proudly.

"Da," Stellan said, "I still have one question. If we do get through the maze and we do get to the Den of Forever Frost, how will we find the key?"

Svern took a long time to answer. "You understand that I have never made it there. But I think if one does, you must first find the quiet in your soul. It will be dim after so much brightness of the ice. You have to move around within this quiet, in this new dimness, and let it talk to you. Let it speak, and you shall find the key."

"But dimness can't speak," Jytte said.

"If you are ready it will. You will all hear it or feel it in different ways. And then you will know where the key is. It will come to you as quietly as a gillygaskin and whisper in your ears." He touched the place on his head where his own ears had been.

CHAPTER 28

A Few Good Bears

The cubs were determined, and over the next few days they improved in their use of a number of different weapons. Svern set up a diagram for them of a hagsfiend, as well as one of a dragon walrus.

"As one might guess, a hagsfiend has a very small heart, and it is located in an almost inaccessible place for attacking with a sword, or a dagger for that matter. There are, however, two points of great vulnerability for a hagsfiend. First there are the eyes. It's from their eyes, as I explained earlier, that they can spin the deadly webs, the fyngrots, that paralyze their victims. If you shoot an ice splinter through their eyes, it can penetrate straight to their peculiar brains, by which they come to their powers of spinning the fyngrots."

Svern drew out a thin rod. "This was crafted to my specifications by a blacksmith who had trained at Bubo's forge. It fits comfortably in a paw. Easy to handle. The other end, as you can see, has a very hollow reed attached, the perfect size for holding an ice splinter. Come outside the den with me, and I'll give a demonstration. You'll see that it is accuracy that counts more than power."

The cubs made their way out of the den. Froya sidled up to her brother.

"Ah, how convenient," Svern whispered in a low voice.

A vole had just stepped out from the roots of a small tree. Svern raised the rod, then flung it forward but did not let go. The splinter, however, whizzed through the air. The vole dropped dead immediately, with the ice splinter planted between his eyes.

The cubs were dumbfounded for several seconds.

"That's accuracy!" whispered Third.

"Incredible!" Froya finally exclaimed.

"Not so incredible," Svern replied. "We'll practice. You just have to keep your eyes on the target and use a nice smooth motion when you launch the ice splinter."

Svern demonstrated. "There is a rhythm to this. Raise your forearm, tilting it slightly back, step forward, snap your wrist, and the ice splinter is released. It's a one-two-three count."

The cubs began, each muttering the count. Nothing launched. The ice splinters just dropped to the ground where the cubs were standing. Finally, on the perhaps tenth try, Froya succeeded. The ice splinter sailed out but only made it halfway to the target Svern had set up. She missed four more times after that. But then Jytte, narrowing her eyes and gritting her teeth, launched her splinter. It sailed straight and true to the target.

"Excellent! Excellent, my daughter!"

Jytte's mouth dropped open. The words rang in her ears — *my daughter!* Stellan turned toward her and smiled. For Jytte, the world had just been set to rights.

For the next few days, the cubs practiced with ice splinters. They all eventually hit the mark, but it was Froya who became the most skillful. They all, however, had their specialties. Jytte showed prowess with the ice dagger, Stellan with the sword, and Third with the bow and ice arrows. In addition to their weapons, Svern had provided them goggles with specially ground ice. He cautioned that they must wear them at all times, for the radiance of the maze could scorch their eyes.

"When we are through the maze and in the Den of Forever Frost, we can put them aside. In the old days it was common to encounter old bears who had somehow lost their goggles and gone blind. So we always wear them even when we sleep."

But it was not all training with swords and ice splinters. In addition, Svern had prepared a map that showed the surest pathways through the maze, which he insisted they memorize. The map also showed a beach beneath a cliff. Somwhere in the cliff was a slot that led to the Den of Forever Frost.

"There is only one entrance into the maze and one exit out of it. However, there are eighteen true paths through it and five hundred false paths. So you must find the true paths that lead out of the maze to the Den of Forever Frost."

"Why eighteen?" Froya asked.

"There are eighteen brightest stars in the Great Bear constellation. A clan was named for each of these stars, and so there were eighteen clans with one representative from each to the Bear Council in the days of yore. We can carry a map with us. But it is important that you memorize the map in case you lose it or we get lost and lose one another."

"These maps," Stellan said slowly, studying the large one that Svern had spread on the floor of his den. "Do they show the hyrakiums?"

"Unfortunately, not precisely. The shaded areas show the known ones. But things have shifted over the centuries in the maze. Not the true paths but the bone pits. Some of these regions have broken off and slid elsewhere. It's similar to when old ice bergs with rotten ice will split and set new floes adrift. Only it's not simply cubs of rotten ice. It's monsters from the yore. Relic creatures who are thought to be extinct. They are no longer on earth, but beneath the earth they lie in wait to devour whatever comes their way."

❧

It did not take the cubs long to master every weapon. They felt at home in the winter den. The evenings were cozy. They began using their weapons for gathering food, although Svern felt that weaponless kills made the prey tastier.

"I can't explain it," he said one night as they consumed a marmot that Third had brought down with his bow and arrow. "I just prefer paw-killed prey. The other materials get in the way. Interfere with the flavor."

On the seventh evening, Svern stepped outside the den and looked up at the sky. The old moon, the one the bears called the Moon of the Ice on Ponds, was just a sliver. The owls called this the Moon of the Copper Rose, and the wolves called it the Moon of the Caribou. He turned to the cubs.

"The moon is slivering; by tomorrow night it will be gone. A perfect night for our mission to begin. We must leave tomorrow night. Even with your goggles, one can only travel through the ice maze on the darkest night before the second sliver of the new moon rises or you risk blindness. So now we must rest up through this night and into the day. You'll need your strength."

That last night, there was little chatter in the den. They were all unusually subdued, each with their own thoughts. Stellan tried to imagine their mission and what exactly lay ahead. Could they thread their way through the ice maze safely without awakening these monsters? Would Jytte and Froya be as deadly with the ice splinters as they had been in practice? Froya had brought down a vole, but a monster? Could an ice splinter mortally wound a hagsfiend?

Jytte had reveled in the music of the word *daughter*, and soon Svern called Stellan son. She wished that her mum were here to hear him say it. Jytte yawned sleepily and tried to remember the softness of her mother's belly fur. Was there anything so welcoming? "Mum," she whispered into the darkness.

Svern looked at them as they drifted off to sleep. He could not help but wonder how it had happened that he, who never had any interest in cubs, had grown attached to not only his own by blood but the other two as well.

Svern was restless and decided to go out and walk around a bit under this last sliver of moonlight. He had not gone far when he came across a distinctive track. He put his muzzle close to the ground — a familiar scent. An evil scent. It could not be. Dark Fang!

CHAPTER 29

Think Like a Bear!

Svenna was in charge of serving tea to certain high-performing members of the Court of Chimes who gathered occasionally in the Mystress of the Chimes's den. These were coveted invitations. She would serve the special smoked Gilraan tea that supposedly was reserved exclusively for the highest-ranking members of the Gilraan.

"Just a taste. And kindly don't mention it outside my receiving den." The Mystress of the Chimes's eyes would glitter as she said this. Svenna saw right through it. It created a sense, albeit a false sense, of intimacy. If the guests had any secrets, he or she might disclose them at this point.

The Grand Patek had become obsessed with the possibility of spies both within the Ice Cap and without. There were rumors of infiltrators from across the Nunquivik sea who had arrived to undermine the Timekeepers. Inside the Ice Clock gossip of snitches, betrayers, and double agents swirled like snow fleas in the Dying Ice Moons.

A paranoid atmosphere was developing. Certain corridors were closed off. Every bear lived in a state of fear. Yet in some ways this condition made Svenna more fearless. She began to plot her own escape.

She went through the panel to the tunnel more frequently, as she was still haunted by the mysterious sound. At first, it'd sounded like the trickle of meltwater, but it'd grown into a low growling. There were four or five places where the sound was more perceptible. She had begun to make a mental map of these spots and tried to figure out the meaning. She reviewed in her head what she knew of the Ublunkyn. It was basically rock sheathed in ice. Now, if the ice began to melt, one might hear the trickle or the flow. Was that growling part of the flow, the movement of the water? And if so, where was it flowing? Into a kind of *bungvik*? If it was being collected in one of these subterranean reservoirs, it was frightening to think of the power it could unleash.

She thought of her daughter, whose ice-gazing abilities had become obvious by the time she was two moons old. What would an ice gazer make of these strange walls?

Perhaps there were other quirks or oddities in the ice through which she could escape. Every entrance to the clock was guarded. But could she swim out through some submarine portal? The seals used these for their work and yet they had never escaped. However, she suspected they were tethered when they dived.

But then she thought of that perplexing noise. Might she drown if she accidentally swam into a bungvik? Nevertheless, she refused to give up hope. There were more pathways and passages to explore. Ghylls — the old Krakish word came back to her — that was the name for secret passages in the Northern Kingdoms.

So it was with the notion of finding more ghylls that Svenna set out shortly after she had served tea in the Court of Chimes. The Mystress of the Chimes had told her that she would be working very intensely in the court on that day and well into the evening going over some new pendulum-arc equations. "I think we are close to a breakthrough!" she announced gaily.

This was perfect. Ever since Svenna had decided to look for ice oddities, especially the ones that might lead to a submerged portal, she had just been waiting for enough time. Now she would have that time — at least ten hours, fifty-three minutes . . . *Oh, don't do this, Svenna!* a voice in her head rebelled. *Think like a bear, not a clock!*

CHAPTER 30

Dark Fang

Svern's nose wrinkled as the shocking scent of Dark Fang, the Master of the Black Ice Ort, permeated the air. This was the bear who had torn off his ears with that poisonous, nearly black fang. Dread began to build in him as his mind returned to the black ice ort. The smell of blood, the shrieks of bears being tortured. How could Dark Fang be here in Uthermere in the Northern Kingdom of Ga'Hoole?

Even after all this time, Svern could still see Dark Fang's face, crisscrossed with a web of scars. Behind the scars, his eyes glowed red. But perhaps most frightening of all was the fang. He had been "gifted," it was said, with that one exceedingly long tooth, which was rumored to be poisonous and as deadly as the venom of a frost viper.

Svern had fallen unconscious when Dark Fang tore off his ears. When his head cleared, he was more determined than ever to escape the black ort. He feigned unconsciousness, pretending to struggle for breath, and then when the guard bent over him, Sven had slashed out with his paw and ripped his neck.

Svern was sure that his escape had damaged Dark Fang's reputation. It must have infuriated the Grand Patek. Dark Fang must have come back to redeem himself, and this time, he would take more than Svern's ears. He would rip out his heart.

Still, Svern never believed that Dark Fang would track him to this remote spot. While a savage fighter, the bear was a mediocre hunter at best. He was not quick on land nor agile in water. But there was no time to ponder how Dark Fang had found him. Svern had to act quickly if he were to get back in time to join the cubs on their mission. But then a chilling thought made him freeze in his tracks. With Dark Fang on his tail, Svern could accidentally betray his den or the entrance to the Den of Forever Frost. Dark Fang would undoubtedly pick up not just Svern's scent but that of the cubs. All would be lost. He must finish this bear here and now. *I am not simply fighting for my own life, but for Jytte, Stellan, Third, and Froya.* The dread receded as his mind clicked into action.

There was no time to waste, yet Svern had to be careful, not careless. He used an old trick that he had learned from other Yinquis to disguise their smee holes, the listening posts that were vital for their spying. He was determined to confuse Dark Fang by laying down a false track that led directly away from the den. This took a while, but he was soon ready to move on to the second part of his strategy.

It was a simple evasion tactic. He first found a sticky spruce tree. The sap flowed freely this time of year, and he broke two of the bushiest spruce boughs and stuck them to his feet and paws. There would be a double advantage here. His own scent would be disguised by the strong-smelling sap and his footprints erased by the bushy needles of the limb.

There was little time to do all this, however. Dawn was about to break. The lighter it became, the easier it would be for Dark Fang to find him. He just had to hope that the cubs would not panic when they awakened and discovered his absence. They'd have to set off without him. There was such a slim window of time when it would be safe for them to pass through the ice maze in the Den of Forever Frost. Scraping out a rough map on the floor of his den the previous day, he had shown them the route they needed to follow to get to the entrance. He just prayed that they would not linger but go ahead. Time was of the essence. This he had drummed into their heads. He knew it would be a shock for them to find him gone, but they simply must trust that he would meet up with them between the slivers of the moon to enter the den.

❧

By late afternoon of the following day, he had walked countless leagues. Dark Fang's scent had dissolved. Surely the cubs had left for the cliffs by now. He had forgotten how quickly the days began to shorten this time of year. The last sliver of the old moon was sailing overhead when he began to get an odd sense that perhaps he was being followed, although he caught no scent. He had to change his direction. He walked on for several hours.

Then, emerging from a stand of birch trees into a clearing, he saw a shape. The shape cast a shadow. How on this nearly moonless night could a shadow be cast? The shape slid toward him.

A voice slithered out of the night. "I've been expecting you, Svern."

CHAPTER 31

Slivers of the Moon

"I think we have to accept that fact that he's gone," Stellan said wearily. They'd been searching for Svern for hours, but there was no sign of him.

"Gone? What do you mean, *gone?*" Jytte asked, scowling at Stellan.

"Just what I said. Svern has left us."

"He'd never do that!" Jytte scoffed, but Stellan could see the panic in her eyes.

He wouldn't just leave, Jytte told herself. Her father, her father who had called her daughter. Why would he abandon them again? Had she dreamed that they had become so close? That he really might love her, care for her? "He'll come back. I know he will. We just need to wait a bit longer."

"We *can't* wait," Stellan said. "We are between the last

sliver of the old moon and the first of the new. If we don't leave now, we'll be blinded in the ice maze even with our goggles."

"You want to go *without* him?" Jytte asked, staring at her brother in disbelief. "Are you crazy?"

"This is our mission, Jytte. This is what we have planned for since we left the Nunquivik." Stellan's voice was rising. "We have to destroy the clock and rescue our mum before it's all too late. Before the bears of the Ice Clock destroy this world. Don't you get it?"

"Everyone, calm down," Third said, struggling to keep his own voice steady. He knew Jytte was on the verge of panic and he was as bewildered as she was. "Let's see if he took his dagger, his ice sword, his goggles."

"Good idea!" Jytte said. If his weapons and tools were gone, it meant that Svern was planning to meet them on the beach. He had shown them this spot on a map. It was just below a slot in the cliffs that led to the Den of Forever Frost.

"I'll go look," Froya volunteered, then scampered off to the armory dens. She returned a few moments later. Her crestfallen face said it all. "His shield, his goggles, ice sword, and dagger are still there."

A stunned silence followed. "Something must've happened to him," Jytte said as a sickening feeling began to flood through her. "That's the only explanation."

Stellan shook his head. "No," he said softly. "I'm sorry, Jytte, but it's far more likely that he decided to leave. We must get our weapons and go with or without him."

"But, Stellan," Jytte said in a voice that threatened to break into a sob. "Why would Da have taken the trouble to train us only to leave us now?"

"Maybe that was his plan all along. Maybe he thought he wasn't up to it. That he would be a hindrance, imperil our mission. He's a good teacher but maybe not such a great warrior anymore. He didn't want to be a risk for us."

"I think we should wait," Third said suddenly.

"We can't wait. We have to leave now," Stellan said through clenched teeth. "We have to get to the den on the edge of darkness. Remember what Svern said. Darkness is our friend in that glaring place. Even with goggles, we can't risk blindness. With the passing of the first moon slivers our chances are —"

"Zero," Jytte finished for him. "He knows how dangerous this is. That's why he insisted on coming with us. He's on his way back, I just know it." Their father would never willfully abandon them.

Froya looked between the arguing bears.

"I . . . I . . . I'm sorry, Third, but I think that Stellan is right. We must go. Go now!"

Third nodded slowly. He knew that it cost her a lot to disagree with him. He didn't mean for her to have to choose sides. He regretted having put her in this position. But if there was one thing that was most important for this mission, it was that they all agreed. They were in it together — all four of them. It was one for all and all for one. There was no other way if they were to succeed.

And so they went.

Between the slivers of the two moons, the cubs swam out of the firth to where the sheer rock wall of a cliff plunged straight down to meet the water. Jytte was filled with sadness and disbelief. She imagined her father dead or terribly wounded. But perhaps he had simply left because he thought he would be a hindrance to their success. Stellan was just perplexed. He did his best to banish thoughts of his father as the victim of some dire catastrophe. And yet he couldn't imagine anything else.

They walked down the pebbly beach that had a dusting of snow and found the fallen tree Svern had mentioned. Just behind its upturned roots was the cliff face with the slot.

"Remember Da said we have to start off single file or we won't fit without shields," Stellan reminded the cubs.

Jytte looked around forlornly. *Where could he be?* "Can't we wait just a minute?"

"No more than a minute, Jytte," Stellan replied. "Look how fast the moon sliver is climbing in the sky. It's almost to the tip of the star in Fighting Bear's sword." The threat of blindness was real if they couldn't take advantage of the night that was coming soon.

Jytte swallowed hard, trying to stifle a sob that rose from deep inside, then nodded. It was time to go.

One by one they entered the slot in the cliff. The last to go was Stellan, who turned one more time in hopes of seeing their da swim out of the firth and climb onto the beach. But there was only darkness.

"Don't forget the goggles!" Stellan called, remembering what Svern had told them. *You can't find your way if you're blind. You can't fight if you can't see. Your goggles are as important as your weapons!* And so now they paused and pulled down their goggles as the passageway began to grow brighter.

After a short time, the pathway widened and the cubs no longer had to go single file. The gray of the rock began to fade and crystals of frost crept across it until there was not a patch of rock left.

Jytte stopped and blinked. Something about the goggles made her feel cut off from any world she had ever known. It was as if she had been flung suddenly into a world bristling with frost crystals that floated eerily around her. In some moments it was hard to tell if she was right side up or upside down. She might as well have been floating in space on some remote star. But it wasn't really a star and she wasn't exactly on it, but trapped within it. "I feel as if I am in the very center of a huge ice crystal," Jytte murmured as they moved forward into a more open space.

Third stopped abruptly. "Is this ice or light?"

It was both. But there was a terrible sense of disorientation as the cubs were caught in a crossfire of radiant beams. Shards of ice and light collided. It was impossible to tell if one could move ahead freely without being blocked.

"We can't lose one another," Stellan said. "We must link together and hold on to one another's tails."

"I wish we had real tails like some animals and not just these little fluff balls to grab on to," Jytte muttered.

"You have to work with what you got," Third said stoically. "And I've got the shortest tail of any of you. So I'll go last."

They proceeded. Even with the goggles, the constant brilliance seemed to wear away their perceptions of distance and depth. They would often bump into huge shards of ice, or take a wrong turn.

It was exhausting navigating through the ice maze. And though they were not sleepy, they needed to pause and rest, but only briefly and always careful that their camp was nowhere close to a hyrakium, as shown on their maps.

At one of these camps, Jytte listened to the other cubs snoring softly. She couldn't understand how they could fall asleep in the inescapable harsh brightness. The light was so glaring that even with eyes shut beneath her goggles she felt she could see right through her eyelids. The inside of those lids was a bright pink — pink and transparent.

However, despite the brightness, Jytte felt herself growing tired and at the same time oddly alert. The pink on the inside

of her eyelids began to dissolve into a yellow glare. She felt something brush her shoulder, then pull at her goggles. She was
conscious yet unable to move. Nor could she shout for help. Her
mind was alert yet her body felt dead and she could do nothing
about it. She was desperate to warn the others, but the words
were strangled in her throat. She wanted to put her paws across
her face and hold on to her goggles. They were slipping. But she
could do nothing. Suddenly a sound whistled through the air.
Jytte felt something collapse on top of her. There was a crushing
weight, heavier than anything she had ever felt, that threatened
to squeeze every breath of air from her body.

Jytte was barely aware of Froya pulling her free. She heard
a brittle noise — crackling sounds.

"Is she alive?" It was a voice, an anguished voice — her
brother.

"She's alive. She's breathing," Jytte heard Froya cry out.

Jytte sat up and looked about. She was surrounded by
splintered bones. "Was I sleeping on a hyrakium?"

"A single hagsfiend," Third said hoarsely. "And Froya got
it." He nodded toward a skull with an ice splinter deeply embed-
ded in the eye socket. Yellow goo like a broken egg yolk spilled
from the socket.

Jytte stood up. "It's strange. I'm sure I felt hags' feathers brush
me but there are only bones here. It was so real . . . so real. It
was as if I had been caught in a fyngrot."

"Let's not camp anymore," Stellan said, his voice crack-
ing with fear. He took a deep breath and seemed to recover

somewhat. "I looked at the map. We should be on one of the true paths." He paused, then spoke in barely a whisper. "I sure hope so," he said, looking back at the bones and the yellow pool of the fyngrot.

CHAPTER 32

Shattered

In the forest clearing, Dark Fang peeled back his lips to reveal the immensity of that single fang.

"Well, here I am," Svern replied evenly. "You see, I didn't die. I didn't succumb to the venom in that stupid tooth of yours." Dark Fang growled and bunched his shoulder muscles as if he were about to charge.

Svern's mind moved swiftly. *I am weaponless, not an ice splinter on me, let alone a dagger, and that fang is like a dagger dipped in venom.* But Svern had his wits and speed, undeniable speed, while Dark Fang was a witless, slow-moving beast. *I must get him to charge.*

Svern might have lost his ears, but he had not lost his feet. He rose onto his hind legs and began to dance — fight dancing, his uncle Svali called it. *It's all in the footwork, young'un, all footwork. You get the footwork right, then you can jab and punch. You won't even need an ice sword.* He hoped that was true now.

Svern began to move lightly and quickly across the forest floor. An old pattern came back to him — skip . . . hop . . . hop . . . skip. He was covering a great amount of distance quickly. He'd closed the gap between himself and Dark Fang within a second or two. Then he would pivot and slide out of Dark Fang's strike range.

Within the first minutes, Dark Fang had lashed out with his forepaws a dozen times but not landed a single punch. The bear was tiring. Svern thought if he played this right he might end it quickly with a single punch. Leading with his foreleg, he would close the distance between them, then bounce back on his hind leg, pivot, circle back, and accelerate. Dark Fang's frustration was mounting. He was becoming increasingly confused. Svern would come tantalizingly close but not close enough for the bear to land a punch, and still Svern had not yet swung his paws.

Dark Fang was being taunted by this dancing bear. Rage began to engulf him. He felt mocked. He was the inflictor, the inflictor of pain. This was not how it was supposed to work. And what he didn't realize with each passing second as he was consumed with his rage and frustration was that Svern was edging him closer and closer to a precipice.

But then suddenly Svern felt claws rake his face. Blood spurted into the air. At last! Dark Fang yowled gleefully and raised his paws in triumph. Svern's vision was blurred by blood pouring from his brow but, disregarding his wound, he lowered his head and charged. He smacked the bear in the chest, and the yowl turned to a screech as Dark Fang plummeted over the edge of the precipice.

Panting in the noonday sun, Svern wiped the blood from his eyes and peered down. Dark Fang's body lay broken and tangled on the floor of the ravine. Blood was spreading across the rocks and on one rock he saw the fang — shattered like fragments of black shale, the very kind of stone that smithies used for putting an edge on a blade.

Svern sighed and sat on the edge of the cliff, feeling something release inside of him. He had finally vanquished this sadistic bear. He touched the spots where his ears had been. He touched the patches on his body where his fur had been burned away. This evil was gone.

He looked up at the sky, bright and blue, and thought of the cubs. It was too late to catch up with them. In a matter of hours the second sliver of the new moon would be rising. If they had left when they should have, they would be well into the ice maze by now. *Will they make it?* This was his first thought. Then, like a shadow sliding across his heart, there was dread: *Will they ever forgive me? . . . My son, my daughter, will they ever forgive me?* He fell to his knees and looked up at the great constellation for which the clans had been named. "Oh, Ursus!" he bellowed. "Protect my cubs!"

CHAPTER 33

A Monster Rises, A Star Falls

"We've been here before!" Stellan cried out in frustration. "*Three times* already." The cubs had taken to notching the ice at certain points to track their progress, but it now appeared they were going in circles. Though not an exact circle. The maze had some parts that were spirals or that coiled about and ran back into each other. There were other regions where the pathways formed interlocking triangles.

"And you know what?" Stellan was shaking his muzzle furiously, as if in utter disbelief. "We are not that far from where we first entered the maze. We've made no progress whatsoever."

Third was shocked by Stellan's outburst. Normally it was Jytte who was the impatient cub, easily frustrated and quick to anger.

"I am sick and tired of looking at my own face every time I

turn a corner. And all of yours as well." There were multiple images of the cubs reflecting back at them. "I reach out to make sure that Jytte has her paw on my tail, and what do I feel? Ice, not Jytte!" Stellan's voice rose. "Are we going to be here forever? Are we going to die here?"

Jytte looked in alarm at her brother. She had never seen him like this. "Calm down, Stellan," Jytte pleaded.

But the word *calm* seemed to anger him more. "I swear I'll kick the place down."

"Don't!" Third cried. But the big cub kicked the ice with his immense hind paw. Fragments broke from the wall.

"Well," Jytte said. "You certainly put a notch in that one."

Suddenly the cubs felt a quake in the ice beneath their feet. A crack opened and something began to emerge. A *skull*, Jytte realized, staring in terror. A moment later, bones of a flipper sprang from the crack and scattered. But within seconds the flipper bones started to knit together. Long tusks, twice as long as those of a toothwalker, were reaching toward them from the crack. The cubs backed up against the ice wall as the tusks crept toward them. The skull rolled and suddenly flames shot out from its nostrils. Jytte winced at the heat, then flattened herself against the ice wall, watching transfixed as more bones emerged.

A sulfurous scent filled the tunnel as the cubs could do nothing more than watch in fascinated horror as the scramble of bones continued to fuse, becoming whole skeletons. Patches of skin began to cover the bones. The stench was overpowering.

It was a smell of death and long decay. *I caused this*, Stellan thought. *I caused it! And I shall end it.*

Stellan drew his short dagger and his war hammer. "Aaarrrgh!" he bellowed. In one leap he jumped over the dragon walrus's head.

His reflection had multiplied in the infinity of the mirror maze, but the dragon walrus had no reflection and could only see the multiple ones of Stellan. It was impossible for the monster to tell where he was in relation to the numerous reflections of the cub. This was to Stellan's advantage, and he managed to creep up behind the beast.

The other three cubs watched, spellbound. They heard the slam of the war hammer. The skull smashed into hundreds of pieces. The flames coming from the snout hissed and flickered out. The rest of the bones began to rattle and splinter, then slid away into the crack from where they had emerged.

The cubs looked at one another in amazement.

"It's gone," said Jytte, peering down at the shards of shattered skull. How had her brother done this?

Third wondered if the fragments of skull might somehow reassemble. He was breathing heavily. He reached for his short dagger, ready to smash the piece to dust.

"I'm sorry," Stellan said hoarsely. "I'm so sorry."

The cubs fell into a stunned, exhausted silence. They were all breathing heavily and coughing from the horrid stench. Finally, Third spoke.

"I might be a dreamwalker, but no dream I have ever walked through has been as confusing as this. In dreams there are no walls, walls of any kind, ice or rock. But here there are."

"And everything is always white, glaring white," Froya fretted. "Even our skin no longer looks black in this maze." Froya ran a claw through the fur on her arm. Their normally black skin appeared to be a pasty color closer to gray. "That's simply not right," Froya huffed.

"I have an idea," Third said. "If we can retrace our steps back to the entry, then we can begin again and follow the wall." Third placed his paw on the wall next to him. "We must put this paw, our port paw, on the wall always! If we don't see any notches, we'll know at least that we aren't retracing our old steps."

"I suppose that makes sense," Jytte said.

Froya shrugged. "We might as well try it."

Stellan remained silent. He didn't feel he was in a position to judge anything after having reawakened a monster that nearly killed them all.

"Let's do it," Jytte said.

None of the cubs were thrilled to start over, but they followed Third's instructions and soon arrived at the entrance to the maze.

"Great Ursus!" Stellan exclaimed. "I think it took us forever to get to the notched wall, and we got back here in no time at all."

"This is good, very good," Third said, nodding his head. "It's always helpful to have a method."

"I think we're really on our way now," Jytte said.

Their spirits improved, they set off again, walking briskly and keeping their port paws steadily on the port wall.

⌀

It was Jytte who noticed it first, but she hesitated to say anything until she was certain. She sensed a change. The light, the very air seemed different. It was as if the brittle radiance were dissolving. Finally, with her paw still on a wall, she said quietly, "I think we might be here." She slipped down her goggles just enough to expose one eye. She squinted. "We are here!"

"Really?" Froya said. One by one the cubs took off their goggles. A pale lavender twilight suffused the Den of Forever Frost. The spiky brightness was gone. In the ceiling overhead there was a large opening with the stars perfectly framed. The space was bigger than a den, and circular. Ice benches ringed the perimeter. They looked as if bears had sat in them at one time, for they were scooped out slightly, worn away.

Slowly, Stellan began to walk around, stopping to take in every detail. When he had completed the circle, he came back with a look on his face that Jytte had never seen before. An expression of complete awe. He opened his mouth to speak but no words came out.

"Stellan, what is it?"

"This . . . this is where the council of bears met. This is where they sat. This is the Ice Star Chamber in the very center of the Den of Forever Frost. There are eighteen places for eighteen bears, just as Mum told us —"

Jytte interrupted, "One for each of the eighteen stars of the Great Bear constellation and the eighteen bear clans from the long ago, the time of yore."

"It's beautiful!" Third said, his voice full of wonder.

Stellan remembered his father's words. *You must first find the quiet in your soul. It will be dim after so much brightness of the ice. You have to move around within this quiet, in this new dimness, and let it talk to you . . . Let it speak and you shall find the key.*

Stellan touched his own ears and tipped his head back toward the night sky. "Look, the Svree star." Stellan pointed up. He spoke in barely a whisper, as if any word, anything he said too loudly, might shatter the peace, the calm of this place, and that the brightness and the monsters might return.

"It's magnificent!" Third said.

Third, however, was looking not up but across at an opening opposite the one they had just come through. A wraithlike figure was moving toward them in a cocoon mist.

Could it be? Third thought. The figure nodded as if to say, *Yes, it is.*

"Eervs!" he called.

The other three cubs wheeled about. They saw the bear now — a very ancient bear shrunken with age in a pelt that seemed too large for him. To their confusion, the bear was laughing gently.

"Not Eervs." He paused. "Here, I am Svree. It's rather like the mirror maze you just emerged from. Except not an image. It's the reverse of my name. Eervs becomes Svree, here in the den. Welcome to the Ice Star Chamber of the Den of Forever Frost."

CHAPTER 34

"I Can't Die. I Can't..."

For several days, Svenna had spent every spare moment exploring the tunnels, searching for a way out. She might not be as blessed as her daughter was with her gift of ice gazing, but she was learning ice and learning to understand the finer distinctions exhibited by the crystals.

However, nothing looked promising until she stumbled across a wall where the geometry of the crystals seemed quite different. Along the sides of the tunnel, the ice was cratered with small recesses. The recesses were shallow for the most part and lacked the depth of a true cave. But she decided to poke her nose into one. A scent swirled out.

"Blood!" she whispered. "Seal blood."

If there was one thing that Svenna knew, that every bear knew, it was the scent of seal blood. And what she smelled now was the blood of a little blue. The odor had to be coming from somewhere within this shallow cranny.

She poked farther into it. She was about to run her tongue along the sides to try and detect a crack, anything through which blood or the scent of blood could have seeped, when she realized that the ice itself had tricked her eyes.

This must be like the maze ice in the Den of Forever Frost, she thought. The back wall reflected another wall. It was a tight squeeze getting herself into the cranny, but then it opened up into a true ghyll. She began crawling down it on all fours. The scent became stronger, and she picked up another scent as well — fox! How could that be? There were no foxes in the Ublunkyn. For some reason the bears of the Ice Clock did not trust them.

The ghyll twisted and turned. The way became somewhat slippery, and she heard a new sound reverberating: A muffled thrumming noise. The path sloped down steeply. Svenna had to grip with all of her claws so as not to skid out of control. The scent of seal blood and fox saturated the space. The air throbbed with the rhythmic mechanical sound. She started to slide. She could not stop herself. She was careening off the sides of the ghyll. She braced herself to smash into a wall. *Great Ursus!* she thought. She realized that she must be close to the underwater works of the clock. *I shall be chewed up by the gears of the great clock. I shall die. And then it will all be over.*

But there was no crash, only a splash, as Svenna found herself in a shallow pond at the end of her slide down the ghyll. By the edge of the pond on an icy bank covered in blood, a Nunquivik fox bent over an injured blue seal, who was bleeding heavily.

"I thought sooner or later this would happen," the fox said without turning to look directly at Svenna. "That you would find out."

Me? thought Svenna. "You know me?"

"Of course. Grade one numerator in the Oscillaria, first degree with an attachment to the harmonics laboratory in the Court of Chimes." The fox paused. "My court. My lab." The fox turned toward her. The slash of two golden eyes flickered blindingly.

"You're not —" Svenna said, utterly dumbfounded.

"Oh, but I am. Galilya, Mystress of the Chimes."

"So . . . ," Svenna started to say. "It's true. The Ki-hi-ru legends of shape-shifting are true." Svenna almost staggered with disbelief. But it all made sense now. The white pelt, the golden eyes, the Mystress's habit of sleeping with her head facing north.

Svenna watched mesmerized as the fox began to lose its long, luxurious tail. Her shoulders broadened and her entire form seemed to swell. Within seconds she was once again a bear and now crouching over the blue seal.

"He's dying, but he has something to tell you."

"Me?" Svenna said, crawling up the ice bank. The seal's eyes were as blue as his coat.

"My name is Jameson," he said haltingly, gasping for each breath. "I've . . . met . . . your cubs."

"My . . . my cubs?" Svenna could feel her heart beating wildly in her chest. She swayed and dug her claws in deeper to the ice floor to steady herself. "Are they . . . well?"

"They were well . . . when I last saw them. They were well and they have names."

"Names?" she repeated incredulously. "What are they?"

"Jytte and Stellan."

"The skipping stars," Svenna whispered, her voice breaking, tears running down her cheeks. "They are alive."

"Indeed, they were when I last saw them. Some moons ago."

"But how did you know they were mine?"

"Your daughter, Jytte . . ." The seal seemed to have regained some strength. "She looks just like you. And I heard them mention your name — Svenna."

Her heart leaped. "What did they say?"

But the seal did not answer. Could not answer. He'd already used his final breath. Svenna stared with sorrow at the blood-stained ice beneath the seal. "What happened to him?" The seal's wounds had not come from a predator. Bears always had quick, clean kills.

"He was maimed by the gears below the clock," Galilya said.

"And you, why are you here? Who are you — really?"

"A traitor," Galilya said calmly. "A traitor to the clock."

The words shook Svenna to her core. "You, the Mystress of the Chimes, a traitor?"

Galilya sighed. The sigh was touched with sorrow, with regret — two emotions that Svenna thought she would never have believed possible for this bear.

"It's all a deadly nonsense. You see, Jameson and I were trying to stop the clock. Stop it and end this heresy. And prevent another Great Melting."

So much had happened, it was hard for Svenna to process what this puzzling bear — fox? — was telling her. "I don't understand. There's no way to prevent the next Great Melting. The bears here think that praying to the clock will keep the waters at bay, but the clock is a false god. It has no real power."

Galilya nodded. "It is indeed a false god. But the Grand Patek would rather kill every bear in the kingdom than admit that. He feels his authority slipping away — too many bears have begun to doubt the clock's power. And so he's prepared to take drastic steps to prove that the clock is indeed a god . . . a vengeful one."

"How?" Svenna asked, driven by a strange combination of curiosity and fear.

"By opening the bungvik beneath the Ice Cap, of course."

Svenna opened her eyes wide. "Then it is a bungvik."

"How did you figure that out, my dear?"

"I heard what I thought was meltwater. Then I heard something more — a growling."

"Precisely — the submerged baffles and the gears of the clock, herding water into the bungvik. And when the bungvik is opened, there will be a new Great Melting, releasing enough water to drown nearly every creature in the kingdom — except the ones here at the Ice Cap. We would be saved. We, the holiest of holies, would escape."

Svenna stared at Galilya as her mind raced to process this horror. Would the Grand Patek really destroy millions of lives to secure his power?

Galilya continued. "You see, like all tyrants, if he cannot control the entire world, he wants to destroy it. The seeds of true evil sprout in the lust for power. The Grand Patek lusts like no other creature on earth."

"Who knows about this plan?" Svenna asked, her voice trembling.

"The Chronos knew. That's why he was killed. Secrecy was paramount. Freedom dies in darkness. Free will is the victim of ignorance. The clock as a god — hah!" She laughed harshly. "There is no such thing as true faith. Only power. That is what the Grand Patek wants. That is his faith."

She took a deep breath and looked into Svenna's eyes. "You never believed. You are too smart. I saw that from the first day when you arrived. You are 'of Svree,' as the old bears would say."

Svenna's head was whirling. It was as if her whole world for the last countless moons at the clock had been turned upside down, but strangely enough, it felt as if it were coming right side up once again.

"What was Jameson's role?" She looked down on the dead seal. His wounds were deep, and there were dozens of them.

"Jameson was an excellent diver. He would plunge down toward the deepest gears and the baffles that directed the water to the bungvik. But I had a plan that I had been devising for years. And it was a way to slowly, over time, alter these gears and baffles that regulated the water into the bungvik, so that the water would leak out gradually and would not cause the complete catastrophe, another Great Melting, that the Grand Patek envisioned. But Jameson ventured too deep into the mechanisms and suffered grave injuries."

"Why did you come here in the first place?" Svenna asked.

Galilya sighed deeply. "That is a long story. A story for another time. But there was once a bear called Uluk Uluk and I . . . and I . . . I fell in love with him. I became a bear so I could love him. And I did love him until . . ." Her voice broke. "He found out who I really was. But as I said, a story for another time." She cast her eyes down on Jameson. "He was a noble seal." She looked at Svenna. "I'm sorry I have treated you as I have. But you were so bright. I knew I could make good use of you." This sent a shiver through Svenna's fur like the sharp edge of a bitter wind.

"If we can actually stop the clock, we can slow the flow to the bungvik and let it drain off naturally." Galilya tipped her head to one side, as if awaiting an answer from Svenna.

"I want out!"

"But you can't. You are part of my plan."

"Your plan!" Svenna roared. "I am not your plan or anyone else's plan. I'm getting out of here."

"You wouldn't dare." Galilya's eyes turned hard.

"Oh yes. Yes, I would."

Svenna stood up, raised her paw, then smacked Galilya squarely in the face with all her might. The Mystress of the Chimes's eyes briefly flared, then rolled up into her head, and she collapsed.

Svenna looked around desperately. There had to be a way out. There were blood traces from Jameson. She might try following those. Somehow he must have gotten here from the region of deep gears. Dare she go that way if it was the only way out? Even if she was slashed by the gear blades, she was larger than a seal — thicker pelt, thicker skin. She glanced back from where she had come. But could she make it? There was no argument. She would rather die trying than stay another millisecond in this place.

CHAPTER 35

The Spirit of Svree

"So you are Svree," Jytte said, her voice full of awe. Svree who had threaded through all their mother's stories like a golden filament weaving together the tales of the bears: the time of Svree, the council of Svree, the Svree star that guided bears.

"I am the spirit of Svree, the first chieftain of the council of the Den of Forever Frost." The bear paused. "And you are the keeper of the key to the Ice Clock."

"Us?" Stellan said. How could they be the keeper of something they'd never seen? That they only recently learned existed?

A shimmer caught Stellan's eye. A gold key was melting out of the frost crystals on which they stood.

Stellan crouched down, studying the key. It glimmered like a constellation — stars not in the sky but in ice. It seemed to radiate a light that spilled onto Stellan's paws, suffusing him with a sense of duty. Their quest was hardly over; it was just beginning.

"Touch it, lad. Pick it up. It won't run away." Stellan hesitated. It might not run away, but the responsibility was awesome.

"And we can stop the clock with this?" Jytte asked. "You'll help us?"

"Oh, no, I cannot go above the ground, except for that one time where I met you at the Grundensphyrr firth. I'm a spirit, a soul. I cannot even go to Ursulana until the clock is stopped."

"Why is that?" Froya asked. Her brow crinkled in puzzlement.

"My punishment."

"*Punishment?* For what?" Third asked.

"For making the clock."

All four cubs gasped. "*You* made the clock?" Stellan said, stunned.

Svree nodded his head wearily. "What was meant to be simply a tool was turned into a god — a fearsome god by bears who craved power. The clock itself has no power."

"Did . . . did . . . they need cubs, Tick Tocks, to make the clock work?" Jytte asked.

"Never!" Svree said. It was the loudest sound his whispery voice had made so far. "That is something that only a craven, power-mad idiot could conjure up. A demon who did not believe in science or engineering at all, but invented a devilish faith on a massive mountain of lies, deceptions, and falsehoods."

Jytte pictured that towering clock at the very top of the Ice Cap, the Ublunkyn. It suddenly appeared fragile, hollow, as if it could collapse with the slightest nudge.

Stellan picked up the key and looked at it. "So if we stop the Ice Clock, we'll defeat the bears of the Ublunkyn Ice Cap?"

Svree nodded.

"But how do we use the key?" Jytte asked, imagining the daunting task.

"There is a keyhole at the very top of the clock. If you insert the key and turn it, you'll stop the gears."

At the top, thought Stellan. It would be impossible to reach. Doubt flooded through him. They had the key, but what possible use could it be to them?

"At the very top?" Third blurted. "We saw that clock once. It soars into the clouds. How could we ever get to the top? We'd need wings to do that."

"Exactly. Wings," Svree replied.

"What are you saying?" Jytte asked, growing impatient.

"Owls. You must go to the owls of Ga'Hoole. To the Great Tree." He stopped talking and regarded them carefully. "You have met your destiny; now you must carry on. Go to the owls."

CHAPTER 36

The Stars in Their Place

The four cubs climbed out of the Den of Forever Frost through the sky port. They were surprised to find themselves not that far from where they had first entered. The day was ending, the sun slipping away to another world, leaving just a red seam glowing in the distance on the horizon. It was now bitter cold, and sea smoke roiled up from the firth where the cold air hit the warmer water. The smoke writhed and coiled like a vaporous snake. It then began to stretch out into a thin mantle over the water.

"It's him! On the other shore," Stellan cried out.

"Who?" Froya said.

"Svern! He's . . . he's alive."

"He's waving at us!" Jytte said. "But why didn't he come with us?" Her emotions were in a tangle. Had he purposely left them to do this all on their own? Abandoned them for no good reason? There must have been a reason. There *had* to be a reason. Jytte hesitated. She wanted to rush into his arms. *But he left us . . . he left . . .* The words clanged in her head.

Then she held the key high in the air. *Be proud of me, Da. Be proud of me!* The stars were just beginning to twinkle. And the star of Svree twinkled the brightest as it rose out of the sea smoke.

"Look!" Svern cried out. "The skipping stars! Your stars, my daughter, my son!" Jytte felt her heart swell. She grabbed Stellan's paw and squeezed it hard.

And indeed the skipping stars had shot out across the darkening night and seemed now to swing just beneath the pointer star of Svree.

Stellan looked back toward the Great Bear constellation as it lumbered out of the east. "Look, Jytte, the knee star, Svern. It follows the heel star of Mum . . ."

They heard a splash. "Da is coming," Jytte said.

Their father had plunged into the water. Stellan had never seen his father swim. What a beautiful swimmer he was. The water of the firth seemed to part for him. His front paws barely made a ripple. But then Stellan spied an odd curl of water coming off one of his hind paws. *A paw just like mine!*

It only took him a few strokes to cross the firth. He bounded out of the water and rushed toward them. As he gathered the cubs to his chest, they could hear the beat of his big heart.

He licked them all with his great blue tongue as they buried their faces in his wet pelt and rejoiced in the very blackness of his skin beneath that fur.

After several moments, Jytte peeked out from beneath her father's arm.

"The stars are in their place," Jytte whispered as she looked toward the gathering night. "Almost." Then she thought, *But you cannot love the stars without the blackness of the night.* She looked again for the heel star called Svenna.

They all sat out late that evening. After the cubs told a stunned Svern about their conversation with Svree, Svern told of his encounter with Dark Fang.

"I knew it had to be something terrible. That you would never not come," Jytte said.

Despite the daunting task that lay before them — a quest to find the owls and convince them to help the cubs stop the clock — Jytte felt strangely at peace. She tipped her head toward the night sky and relished the darkness, the shadows of the branches that spread across the ground, a pale thin cloud that swept above them. Snow had just begun to fall, as the time of the first of the snow moons was coming.

The cubs and Svern all fell into a comforting silence. It was the kind of silence where one might hear the whispering of the stars, the murmurs of ice crystals forming, or the riffle of a wind through an owl's feathers. It was the silence of all the most elusive mysteries of the universe. It was the silence that binds companions in a long night as winter comes.

About the Author

Kathryn Lasky is the author of over fifty books for children and young adults, including the Guardians of Ga'Hoole series, which has more than seven million copies in print, and was turned into a major motion picture, *Legend of the Guardians: The Owls of Ga'Hoole*. Her books have received numerous awards, including a Newbery Honor, a Boston Globe–Horn Book Award, and a Washington Post–Children's Book Guild Nonfiction Award. She lives with her husband in Cambridge, Massachusetts.

The quest continues in . . .

BOOK 3

Stellan and Jytte have the key they need to stop the Ice Clock. But in order to use it, they'll have to assemble the greatest army Ga'Hoole has ever seen. Can they convince the bears, owls, and wolves to work together before it's too late?